*Crash The Bus*

I0549060

*95%  based on fact -*
*(the other 5% is more reliable)*

*James Murphy*

# Crash The Bus

## by James Murphy.

### © *Heretic's Press* **2015**

All rights reserved.

**Published by The Heretic's Press**
**London**
*www.hereticspress.co.uk*

*By the same author*

*To Hell in a Handcart (play-script)*
*The Poets (play-script)*
*The Misanthropist's Secret Love Life (poetry)*
*The art of Exile (poetry)*
*Handbook for the Damned (cultural & literary criticism)*

*ISBN* **978-0-9567920-6-8**
*Kindle ISBN* 978-0-9567920-7-5
*© 2015*
**The Heretic's Press**
*www.hereticspress.co.uk*

# Crash The Bus

*95% based on fact -*
*(the other 5% is more reliable)*

**James Murphy**

## About The Author

Born in 1957, James Murphy grew up in the suburbs of South London. He graduated in Philosophy from the University of East Anglia at Norwich. He then worked in several different fields (sometimes literally), including journalism and teaching. During the 80s, he lived in Tuscany, and currently resides in Hampshire, where his house has just burned down, as per Nietzsche's Vesuvian exhortation. He has written a play about Nietzsche, *To Hell in a Handcart'*, two collections of poetry: *The Misanthropist's Secret Love Life,* and *The Art of Exile*. He has also written two further plays, *The Poets* and *Disposophobia, as well as a cultural and literary critique, Handbook for the Damned*. He is married with a son.

*Foreword and acknowledgements.*

To Marcus Fellowes warmest thanks are due. The extent to which he has patiently allowed the dramatic twists and turns of his life-story to fall prey to my own wide-ranging, indeed, 'all-licensed' interpretation is the measure of the modesty and generosity of the man.

A couple of years in the writing, with one or two prototypes and false starts, 'Crash the Bus' itself goes back some distance now, and in tracing its path to the creative depot out of which the original concept growled slowly and portentously two or so years ago, I see a companionship that has persisted in fair and foul weather – too much of the latter! – but also one which has deepened over cappuccinos, coffee cake and laughter in abundance. May there be no shortage of the latter in coming years for all of us.

To Jack Murphy, for sharpening my wits against his; indeed, for his unique humour, and for his unstinting, dogged, practical IT help, I offer my delighted thanks!

As regards editorial insight and critical acumen, to Joanna's wit, wisdom, unending good faith and general humanity, I am indebted anew: *Crash the Bus is* dedicated, then, as another small repayment to the one to whom, quite simply, almost everything is due.

## Chapter contents

### PART 1   ---   DESCENT

## PART 2 --- HELL RIDE

*PART THREE – DOWN IN THE SOUL'S BASEMENT*

## PART FOUR – ASCENT

## *Crash The Bus*

*For those who begin to entertain serious doubts
about themselves*

# Part 1 --- Descent.

## 1 – Invitation

*The letter lies neat, singular and pat on the doormat with all the inevitability of fate, but none of the romance.* Please let it be a rejection! Please 'regret to inform' me that on this occasion I have been unsuccessful! Please wish me luck in future applications. But no, something about this letter is bleak: all corporation letters reek of the impending doom of boredom; the fonts they use predict the depersonalised routine, the deadly lack of drama that engendered them. And so, as I collide with the words on the page, my soul crumples with the full impact of the disaster: I have been accepted.

(To be spoken in a nasal monotone:)

"Dear Mr Grant, thank you for your application to take a course as a trainee bus driver with our company, and we are pleased to inform you, etc, etc…"

Stunned, I take the letter into the lavatory, seated nonplussed wherein, I momentarily confuse it for loo paper. If only I could flush away the destiny on offer! But I can't. I desperately need this job. We're broke. Credit cards maxed-out, mortgage repayments in arrears, phone calls from the bank, seedy 'repo men' knocking on the door – the lot. And it's all my fault. Everything is my fault. There's no hiding place from the hackneyed finger of blame. I brought down this poverty on our heads, and there's no mitigation, no diminished responsibility, no deferral of blame onto third parties. It was me. Not my wife, Kate; not her bitch of a sister, not my crazy, junkie mother. And not circumstance. Not society. Not other people's indifference. Not the bloke down the road, not the world and his wife – and certainly not you. Me. I did it. And I've got to make amends. I've got to make it better.

Even now I can hear my six month old son Tom crying upstairs, swiftly followed by my wife Kate's footsteps across the landing to feed him. I hear her distracted call.

'Did it come?' she means the letter, of course, for which we've been waiting dementedly every day for the past two weeks.

'Yes, it came...' I whisper to myself on the loo, which has become my private confessional, my dark sacred stall for disclosing my worst fears.

'Matt, what's the news? Come on, tell me!' Kate emerges from the bedroom with our son attached with infantile voracity to her breast. At least he's stopped crying. I call out from the loo.

'Yes, it's come.'

'Well? What is it?'

'Yes.'

'"Yes" they want you? What, for chrissake?'

'Yes, they want me.'

'Oh thank Christ for that! Hold on!' Kate gently hisses over our son's head. 'Just let me get him down to sleep again. Give me two seconds!'

Strange how, in this post-religious age we still exclaim 'Christ!' when summoning the power of emotional release. In our profound atheism is there still some residual glimmer of an antiquated, religious light which language stubbornly insists on rekindling?

'It's only the interview stage....' I mutter half-heartedly, knowing Kate can't hear; knowing, too, that acceptance by the bus company is pretty much a formality once you reach the interview stage. I survey the cold cup of tea I have distractedly brought into the loo: still I hope this other cup may pass me by too. For this is indeed my cartoon Gethsemane and I have become a caricature Christ in my own garden of trivial agony. I have only a minute or so before I begin to endure a gradual crucifixion by lying - lying every moment of every day from now on: lying to Kate about how pleased I am to get the job, lying to the interviewer I will see, lying to the people I will work with, the passengers I pick up, lying, perhaps above all, egotist that I am, to myself.

I exit the loo as if from a tomb: the shadow of the future falls upon the hall like a shroud. I drift down the corridor like a spirit dispossessed of any capacity for self-determination. I'm a dead man. From now on I will speak these words from the grave of a timetable routine.

A ghost in my own life, I look at myself in the mirror at the end of the hall: I have disappeared. A haunting is about to begin on the drear, grey, litter-strewn, concrete, alienated bus routes of London.

∞

## 2 – When I grow up...

It wasn't always like this. Only a moment ago, or so it seems, I had my feet up on my desk in The City, clicking the 'return' key for daft amounts of money; the next, I'd jacked it all in: the result of an unforgivable attack of conscience that all but killed me – *did* kill me in a manner of speaking; certainly left me for dead that day in Auckland Avenue. But fate is a paramedic: he gives you the kiss of life even when sometimes it might be kinder just to let the patient die.

Then again, given what happened on that, *the* most particular of days, what choice did I have? *Real* choice, I mean, the money-no-object choice exercised by bored billionaires who bowl in and out of the Bond Street of the soul at will. Don't suppose my bus route will go anywhere near Bond Street. Not that I'd want it to. Those shops whose prices burn your eyes are somehow full of poverty.

No, after the event in Auckland Avenue, I had no real choice but to give it - and everything else - up. Not that Ronnie (short, believe it or not, for Ronaldinho; his dad being Portuguese; his mum, from Portsmouth) at the next desk agreed, of course.

'Listen, get that resignation letter back right now! If you jack it in you'll never get another job in The City. Trust me, you know I'm right on this one,' Ronnie added - about everything (more, regrettably, of Ronnie later).

Other friends whose opinions I respected even less warned me not to take what had happened to me in Auckland Avenue too seriously; that it bordered on the reckless to give up the job in this current climate. But then after the event in Auckland Avenue I didn't really recognize my friends anymore. And anyway, if you're bordering on the reckless, why not cross over and investigate the territory? I was, after all, no stranger to its terrain; thanks to a childhood at my mother's finger-nail bitten hands I had learnt "Reckless's" difficult, inflected language reasonably well. In fact, all things considered, I was pretty fluent in the language used by native reckless people.

And then, as I say, after Auckland Avenue what real choice did I have?

Funny: most little boys go through a stage of wanting to drive a bus. No doubt I told my mother just the same as I played with my Corgi toys. 'O my prophetic soul', as Hamlet said about another domestic incident. But then I didn't foresee that the bitch of a bus in question would be the sort that had drunken bastards pissing on me from the top deck at midnight, then falling down the stairs and threatening me with breath rank with beer and curry.

Not that mother would've warned me off any particular career track; no, mother didn't really care about careers as such – apart from her own blind acceleration into the abyss of addiction. My mother was... well, I'd like to say that in spite of everything she was a good person, that I loved her unquestioningly as any kid does, reinforced in my case by a vague sense of our shared isolation; that it was me and her against the world; that dad didn't exist – or to be more accurate, existed only as some weird stranger whom, for reasons never entirely clear to me, I was sent away to, to be scared shitless by twice a year during school holidays.... He wore Cologne that emphasised both his strangeness and our estrangement: - maybe he still does... Dad, daddy. Father.

Anyway, now I'm one myself – but I don't wear Cologne. And I don't scare my son – at least not consciously. No doubt he'll set me right me when he's older – if we're still speaking. Nothing's a given; not even parental love – especially not parental love. My mother. Your mother. The word 'mother'. The power hidden in plain sight in that word to make or mar, despoil or be despoiled. Motherfucker.

## 3 – The silence of waiting-rooms

*Listen to it: all interview waiting-rooms resonate with a certain quality of silence: a silence that heralds the advent of the archangel of insincerity.* For we interviewees are the vocationally insincere, we will say anything to qualify for job-heaven.

Thus I sit, a soul in purgatory bathed in the blanched radiance of strip-lighting perdition. I scan the other interviewees. All colour has drained from our faces, all authenticity from our souls. We are here to impress. And I've never seen a row of less impressive individuals – myself included. Effectively, we form an identity parade, since we have all clearly been convicted of desperation. Thus we await our sentence at the hands of the interviewer. I hear my name called out: the secretary might as well say: 'Will the defendant now rise please.' I stand up from my chair in the dock and step forward to meet my fate. I open the door. Best foot forward – not that I have one. Something in me wants to laugh.

∞

## 4 – The umbilical cord of the past

No, mother was a recurrent train crash - with me as her only passenger, constantly taken in by the company's promise of improved safety standards. Well, I survived my own particular accident of birth – or so rumour has it. Occasionally I still demand an independent inquiry....

Actually, why *is it* so hard to articulate a dislike of one's parents? Some inextricable, indissoluble link between their approval and one's own sense of self-worth, no doubt. If you separate yourself from your parents by consciously disliking them, you can then no longer access the primal sense of value they give you: these two archetypes: the first people who ever loved you, who gave you the confidence that the world is a decent place, one worth getting to know, even joyful, with values you can trust and celebrate. Conversely, to actively dislike your parents is to stand alone, cut off, disinherited from the confidence they give you, the faith in yourself that all real love is based on. In short, if you cut off the credit of parental love then you have to back yourself – but what with? Why is love a commodity we always need to get from an external source? Why can't we supply it to ourselves? Surely the banks in our age have taught us that printed money is not counterfeit?

## 5 – The interview as a surrealist art form

*And we're off!*

'Hallo Mr....' – the interviewer scans my application form again: I want to confirm there has, indeed, been some mistake, but there hasn't.

'Er - Grant... sorry about that, but I've just seen a 'Mr Plant', believe it or not - the rhyme confused me for a moment.' My interviewer's evident ear for a rhyme disconcerts me for some reason. The ice is not broken. I slip on it.

'No problem, it's a boring name – Grant, I mean.'

'Steady on – my name too....' retorts Bus-driver-hirer-man half-smiling without looking up. Indeed, Mr Clive Grant to you! South London Depot manager with special responsibility for hiring and firing lost souls like me.

'Bit different from working in The City – get fed up with all that money, did you?'

And so the game of chess begins with this Knight's leap over my defences. This tricky question puts my king in check - and my interviewer opponent knows it. Whichever way I move I'm vulnerable.

'Not exactly. I fancied a change.' – Too late! Did I really say "Fancy!?"- flippancy is never a good move.

'Well you'll certainly get that here!'

'I mean, I've always liked driving...'

'Don't worry: driving a bus'll cure that!

Thus I go from bad to worse: I now sound like a simpleton. I can feel the straw coming out of my ears. Can he see it protruding? He certainly seems to be peering at me curiously.

Of course, all interviews are ludicrous: everybody knows this - including the interviewers: we all realise the inherent comedy – farce, even, of the roles we're playing out, the attitudes we're striking, the faces we're putting on as part of the show – the expressions we're pulling, gurning as muscularly and mawkishly as children: faces open, faces direct, appreciative; faces honest, faces earnest, faces grave, faces laughing, faces hysterical with sincerity –'watch out, if the wind changes your face will stay that way!' as our mothers used to say. They were right, of course: at the end of the day we do pull a face, and the wind does change and we are left looking the way we look; the wind being experience; the face being your reaction to a life blown away by the stuff. Some brilliant wag said you end up with the face you deserve at forty. What they failed to point out is that you've been busy sculpting it since you were five.

'So, Mr Grant: what makes you think you can drive a bus?' My interviewer's voice is smitten with the curse of a nasal, West Midlands monotone, a dull music rendered deader by decades of dealing with listless 'to-do' lists.

I ponder it long and hard - this, the shallowest of questions I have ever been asked – and thus the most challenging. Bus instructor-interviewer man returns my gaze incuriously from across the desk, and in the airless, colourless, joyless, spiritless, strip-lit backroom of the bus garage time dissolves. He recedes into an unfathomable distance: he could be a million miles way. A desk doesn't just separate two people, it divides time into two: the time before the interview when you were human, and the time after when you became a figure of fun in fate's eyes. Then I deliver my answer.

'Things change. I need the money.'

12

Unfortunately, honesty is the best policy. Mr Grant laughs 'don't we all?' The game of chess simplifies. Mr Grant's knight and my pawns waltz a few cursory steps together, tracing a swift course to mutual victory. For lo and behold! - horror of horrors! - though a letter of confirmation will, of course, be sent, Mr Grant is happy to tell me - off the record - that I can consider myself enrolled on the course. Suddenly the interview's over before it's begun We shake hands. I exit his room smiling into the middle-distance as if lobotomised. I represent no harm to society. That's what *they* think.

∞

## 6 – Golf clubs as defensive weapons

So was there never a moment when I realised there was something wrong with my mother? Not til my best friend Ricky told me his dad had said she was something called a junkie. And it was true; our house was full of junk. Then, clumsily and belatedly, I put the obvious pieces of the tired, old, dysfunctional jigsaw together. In the course of any given day mum would always be suddenly very calm and happy, then slowly very sad and nervous, and she slept a lot - with different men – a few, good, some bad, the vast majority indifferent.

For as long as I can remember there were men passing through the house. Most of them came and went (let's face it, puns have a life of their own); some stayed longer – one in particular stayed far too long. In fact, in the end I left before he did – being literally chased out of my mother's bedroom window by him in a rage. I was, what? - about fourteen, I suppose: I had provoked this particular guy by defending my mother from his attack with a bent old nine-iron. Why my mother, who couldn't stand any sport, kept a battered bag of golf clubs on the landing I can't think. Perhaps, Sybil-like, she had foreseen my need for them. Anyway, he was a dealer. Maybe a pimp. I still think today he would've killed me if he could. Not that my mother would've noticed necessarily...

Ah mother, if only it could've been different..! If only you'd been Princess Grace of Monaco, with me as your little Prince Albert: we could have ponced around on balconies overlooking Cap Ferat together. But you weren't and we didn't.

Anyway, one shouldn't steal other people's fates, it shows a vulgar ingratitude for the largesse of one's own – however subtle, secret and dangled at arm's length the inheritance may seem at times. Moreover, happiness is meant to be in short supply: its rarity confirms its quality; its very unattainability is what makes it desirable. Isn't it precisely the tension of desire that gives gratification such a charge? Is it not our curse to tire of the things we possess? What good would happiness be if we always had it?

## 7 - Dazed in a maze

*The interview done, I exit the dark maze of the depot in a daze. It's stupidly sunny outside.* I see the other men who already do the job: a fair proportion of them are, it's fair to say, fat beyond the call of duty. Perhaps I too will soon be fat, because my thoughts have taken on a uniform weight in contrast to the sunlight. Everything around me suddenly sings the song of uniformity, which is also a threnody for the loss of spontaneity I have just embraced. My life will now be on a timetable, my conscience on a rota. Worst of all, I'll have to wear a uniform. Thus poverty, having crippled me, now seeks to buttress my backbone with stiff, starched trousers and shirt: my soul wears a brace. Without it I will not be able to stand up. I am under the control of its fascist ergonomics (my body seated in a uniform is already like half a swastika). I will even have to wear a badge, my days will be numbered like my bus. A child's voice inside me cries.

∞

## 8 – Over-promotion

'I'm tellin' you: you need you fuckin' 'ead examined,' Ronnie reassured me. 'Have you forgotten what a laugh we have 'ere?' Ronnie did not apparently regard my impending resignation as a lost cause. And it was true: looking back, there had been the statutory number of grotesquely funny times. Truth is, we secretly admire those who transgress on our behalf, and The City is a nexus of gentile transgressions run by numberless pin-striped rogues like Ronnie.

But exaggeration is a vice of mine. Maybe a type like Ronnie is just, as some suggest, a bad apple – a Pink Lady of malfeasance. Let me say straight away: a lot of very decent people work in the Square Mile. Maybe you're one of them. Fate headhunts you. There you were, being witty in the bar after work: step forward good fortune's tribal chief, wearing a - what should have been - tell-tale, sharper-than-average, pale coffee-coloured linen suit, whispering 'there could be an opening with us for someone like you, if you're interested...' One period-of-notice later there you sit: suddenly just a stone's throw away from the Old Lady of Threadneedle Street herself. So what if, close-up, you see she's actually a whore? Who cares if her morality isn't exactly monastic? At least The Square Mile's open about its sewers; its corruption is almost stinkingly honest in an inverse way. Better just to admit it: ambition is a form of social Darwinism. Why shouldn't pleasure be performance-related? Sorry? 'what shall it profit a man if he gain the whole world yet lose his soul?' I'll tell you; starting pay at over £100k basic with all sorts of add-ons, that's what. Ask Ronnie. He knew all about life in the margins.

'I lost two hundred grand with that phone call!' Ronnie leant over and confided to me casually just before lunch. – 'Shorted that Greek olive oil at just the wrong bastard moment!' Never mind, I'll hide it in some pension fund - only til I make it back – promise!'

'Ronnie, should you be telling me this?'

'You're my boss, aren't yer? – At least for now! Anyway, make it back this afternoon. No problem!' Was Ronnie joking? Who knew? Not me. Who cared? Not me. As I say, Morality in investment banks is a grey area. It blends with the décor.

What is it about offices? Can the mere influence of a physical environment induce nausea over time? If one's mind drinks in too much steel and glass does it make one cold and clinical inside? I had particularly come to hate the toweringly expensive 'house-plants' and even more massively expensive, trashy abstract art with which the bank affected to mask its clinically minimalist entrance hall.

Not that such trivial irritations weighed one whit as my impending resignation hung in the balance of my conscience; nor did I suffer any guilt about the money I made: far from it: I could stand the cash - or so I thought. Then again, maybe the cash couldn't stand me. Maybe behind my back, money had taken a pathological dislike to me and was plotting to kill me? Money is cunning. It masks itself in moral support, whilst all the time, behind your back, it hates your guts.

No; 'Geld macht frei', it should have said above the swanky swing doors as we traipsed into work, into our concentration camp of money, each day. Were we, then, guards or inmates? Either way, our souls seemed starved of a certain kind of nourishment, our faces thin and grey, our uniforms, too, were pin-striped; our crucial difference being one of pain. We felt none. We left that

17

to the punters whose money we gambled with, whose trust funds Ronnie rifled. The good, old, innocent punters investing their trust in us – and their own naivety. During lunch, still undecided, I went and got my resignation letter back to buy a bit more time.

### 9 – Insomniac report at 2.38. a.m.

*I can't sleep. Insomniac, way past midnight: having got the bus-driving job, an eerie, drug-like silence has descended on the flat.* Kate is deeply asleep next to me. You could hear a pin drop – not that pins ever do drop: who ever saw a pin drop? Pins, stray pins, are mysterious loners, vocational: to be dropped is, where a pin is concerned, to have a holy mission, a calling: as such they just appear miraculously on the floor – actually, out of the floor: that's what these special pins are for; and you pick them up and all the day you don't have good luck. Dropped pins have nothing to do with luck; dropped pins exist solely to be analogous to silence – and the implication of silence, which, in this case, is the decision I've made to surrender to fate and my grotesque new role as a trainee bus driver.

And now Tom is awake again. - You could say the sound of insomnia is a baby crying in the night.

∞

### 10 – 'Geld macht frei...'

'Here he comes: boss man - late again!'

Nominally in charge of him, Ronnie was only half-joking: he knew right from the start that I'd been over-promoted. I have *always* been over-promoted – indeed, thrust into positions for which my lack of desire to occupy them absolutely unqualified me. Then again, perhaps over-promotion is the working definition of life itself? Life scoffs at our self-satisfaction, our assumption that we are the finished item. Life is one of those annoying superiors who sees the potential in us....

The reality was that Ronnie was in charge of me because, from day-one, and unlike me, he had always known what he was doing at the bank and why he was doing it. Pleasure. Not as a by-product of his career, not as an incidental perk of the job, but as the sole motivating force in his life. Ronnie could teach me a thing or two about this deeply Freudian principle – whether I liked it or not.

Ronnie, in all his stereotypical Latin womanising glory! Ronnie didn't mind being a stereotype. In fact, he loved it. He was so good at it after all, and for better or worse we all love the things we're good at, whether it's shorting stock, meditating, masturbating, holding dinner parties, torturing prison inmates.... In fact, Ronnie was so stereotypical he had taken stereotypicality to new levels of excellence whereby he was no longer stereotypical at all. 'Rubber Ronnie' never at a loss for a prophylactic when the moment came – and he made sure it did at least twice a week (he claimed) and never with the same girl twice.

'Look at her – what a babe – and that one: begging for it.' Ronnie would assure me, gazing out through the café's picture windows at the human cinema of unsuspecting women unreeling before his eyes over coffee.

'Seriously, you must be mental, Matt!' Ronnie based his diagnosis of my insanity upon my pathological marital fidelity and the knowledge that Kate and I were to have a baby in the near future. Well, Kate would have the baby. I would watch.

'You're far too young to start a family! Getting married was bad enough! Jesus, one woman for the rest of your life. You must be joking!'

'Must I, Ronnie?'

'Yeah, forget monogamy! Muslims have got it right: men are naturally polygamous. There's an army of 'em out there! Women, I mean, not Muslims.'

'That doesn't mean to say you have to surrender to them, Ronnie.' I would remonstrate. (Incidentally, I can recommend remonstrating  - it's an alternative to masturbating: subtler and more psychologically rewarding - though, sadly, equally addictive.)

'No, seriously; bottom line: women want sex as much if not more than men. They love it!'

Ronnie thus revealed the ancient fact of woman's delight in her own sexuality as a modern Road-to-Damascus epiphany. But then, as William Blake, the poet, knew, though we *as individuals* may pass through them temporarily, states of mind themselves are timeless; in this regard Ronnie's magically dated from post-war decades when the revelation of woman's capacity for sexual pleasure still possessed the power of taboo.

'That's where I come in! – I answer woman's prayers...'

'We know, Ronnie: you're a god.'

'You know that lovely girl, Lola, the one in 'futures', the one that said she wasn't interested?'

'Yes, Ronnie, I know Lola in Futures...'

'Job done... tits like water-melons!'

'Has she indeed?'

Shamefully, I knew this to be true because one hot night after work last summer, during one of those rare, magical weeks when a Mediterranean wind blows up from the south and suddenly London can be mistaken for Palermo or Madrid, Lola had had drunken occasion to set her water-melon stall out privately before me at closing time, and I had, equally drunkenly, refreshed myself thereat.

Do I then snigger like a schoolboy, resort to sexist objectifications of Lola; descend to making vulgar fun of the traditional seaside picture postcard target, of Lola's wonderful big tits? Far from it. Lola was voluptuous both mentally and physically: she deserved a better lover than me, certainly than Ronnie. My modest point is that Lola's water-melons had indeed been so dauntingly generous in their proportions that one scarcely knew how to acquit oneself of the task of taking them in hand, taking comprehensive care of each of them in turn, as it were, without leaving either feeling neglected. Lola's breasts were, when all is said and done, the work of two men. That said, undermanned as I was, I did my level best to please in difficult circumstances.

The human heart being a pendulum, pleasure swings swiftly back toward guilt (at least in *my* grandfather clock). Subsequently, Lola and I had both thought it best to keep our brief, tropical transaction of said water-melons secret. We both had partners we didn't want to hurt unnecessarily. In this context, guilt can be an adhesive that bonds together the fractured pieces of romance.

And what is it about one-night stands that chills one to the bone? Is lust always ultimately overridden by a desire for the intimacy of love? Is it the corpse-like contact with a stranger's skin that makes one run from the graveyard bed of lust back to the comparative warmth of hearth and home – even if the living soul one dwells with there is not so warm as once she was? Kate, whom I'd known on and off, since I was sixteen, loved me – and I loved her; but in our affair, and separately beknownst to both of us, the time of secrets had begun....

Secrets: their existence cuts both ways, can kill the truth or keep it alive. In Ronnie's case, secrets were indispensable to the survival of human dignity.

'Let me tell you mate, Lola loves it when you ---'

'Ronnie, I've got to make a call, mate...'

What is it about other people's sexual prowess? Why do they think you want to know? I don't even want to know about my own.

But of course, money is the great aphrodisiac - and The City is the arena of sexual prowess. Everywhere you turn there is some mighty warrior or Amazon ready to regale others with tales of their victories over the opposite sex. The women are, so I'm told, no better. Indeed at the top of the tree, the bitch goddess herself, Naomi Hunter, Queen of Credit Default Swaps – including an option on yours! - Are you man enough? Fortunately not. But I'm running ahead of myself....

### 11 – All romance ends up in the sound of a baby crying

*It's now three-twenty a.m. - in five hours I'll be behind the wheel of a bus! If I don't get to sleep now I'm lost. And Tom is still crying - suffering from colic.*

It is said that a baby crying is meant to be the most alarming sound a human can hear. Any parent will vouch for this evolutionary truth. There's nothing like the sound of infantile crying to rupture human concord. One's instinct is to lash out - blame each other immediately. After all, crying is such an extreme thing to do; the action itself so devoid of grace and style, of pride and status – is this why we adults unlearn to cry? No, you don't cry unless you really, really have to: unless, for example, the big end of your ice-cream has plopped onto the floor, or mummy stops you pulling out teddy's eyeballs just when you were getting somewhere. But this is of course further down the line. A baby's crying is far worse.

When you have a baby, everything changes. The word 'everything' has four blood-stained syllables, and not a mother or father but the holy claret in their veins drains out over every one of them. Say it slowly: 'E-ver-y-thing'…. In the dark aegis of this one word, black becomes white, day turns to night. Nothing is what it seems - in spades. (which morph into hearts and back into clubs in the blink of an eye – nor, contrary to whatever James Bond might have you believe, are the diamonds forever).

Try it: have a baby. Suck it and see. Overnight, the young woman you loved, the woman you took away on romantic trips to the Amalfitana coast; the woman you wined and dined by Mediterranean candlelight; the woman you dazzled with your wit and wisdom; the woman into the cool waters of whose eyes it was once your beautiful delight to dive... and dive again, baptising yourself anew in their sensual depths; overnight, that same woman becomes an exhausted, washed-out, gaunt, ghost of the person you knew before - a hag of temporary unhappiness.

Even the long hard months of pregnancy don't prepare you for what happens when another human being emerges from the body of the woman you love. But then maybe you should have known; maybe you just didn't bother to look properly and notice that she was being taken over by a very weird reality, one which swells her body with its rapacious intent. Pregnancy is the one form of parasitism we willingly embrace. But what did you think was growing inside your wife if not the colossal, unstoppable force of change? Did you think that just by giving it a name, by labelling this primal, elementary power Jack or George or Helen or Hattie that you were somehow in control of the process; that you were the one in charge of the whole monstrous beauty of birth? The gods laugh as mortals make (family) plans.

But the woman you love? Couldn't she tell? Didn't she know that something cataclysmic had occurred in her body? An epoch-making event, like the crashing of a comet onto the earth's surface, heralding the extinction of a whole way of life? The trail of a comet is the shape of the sperm, which lands with similar effect in the womb of a woman: life careers back to earth and her – and your - landscape is changed forever, and your old selves are dinosaurs whose day, unbeknownst to them, is done.

In truth, the woman you love knew something fatal was afoot the moment she knew her period was suspiciously late. That trivial test of bodily catastrophe she bought in Boots; that slow instant in time the paper took to turn violet simultaneously confirmed her worst fears and best hopes. - If women multi-task better than men, maybe that goes for their emotions too. Pregnancy besieges the woman you love with ambivalence: a wave of quiet ecstasy in the fulfilment of her bodily purpose crashes against the rocks of sudden angst at the enormity of the task confronting her; absolute hope beats its head against a shabby wall of blank despair; a pride in a sudden womanly coming of age tips over into a momentary melancholy at the loss of girlhood; a vital strength gained through an acceptance of responsibility for a defenceless baby's life is dimmed by a weakening of resolve in the light of the impending loss of her own personal freedom. – The woman you love knew all these things: even if she didn't articulate them as crudely as words necessitate, she knew them all the same. But she didn't tell you; didn't confide everything to you – because she knew you wouldn't've  - couldn't've - understood. How could you, a mere male, be party to such violent wisdom? Were not the Eleusinian mysteries an eternally female affair for a reason? Are they not still? – Neuter them in our modern innocence as we would, do not some secrets of sexuality remain germane (no pun intended) only to each gender?

Three-thirty a.m. Suddenly Tom has stopped crying. The house holds breath....

∞

## 12 – In praise of stereotypes.

And so what if Ronnie was a stereotype? What's wrong with being a stereotype? 60,000 people jumping for stereotypical joy when a stereotypical footballer kicks a stereotypical ball into a stereotypical net seem happy enough! Or 20 million people watching Coronation Street. No, I see satisfied stereotypes all round me: grabbing stereotypically quick low-calorie salad lunches, exchanging stereotypical opinions about Far-Eastern markets or the crisis in the Middle-East, washing them all down with stereotypical Americanos, maybe slipping in a stereotypical game of squash before going back to stereotypical offices where they make stereotypical deals, have stereotypical affairs, and go back to stereotypical cuckolded husbands, cheated-on wives. This sounds bitter, but isn't. I'm just saying that if the pattern of our more or less uniform days shapes our souls, then most follow a regimented, stereotypical course; and that these stereotypical destinations of office, home and holiday seem to do just fine, thank you.

Only they don't. Not really. Sameness eventually calcifies. Unobserved by us, our deepest feelings drip in slow, single tear drops; leave a deposit over time. The soul is a cave full of sentiments as old as stalactites. And who hasn't longed to smash a stalactite? No, we yearn to break the mould. Fortunately for society only some of us are dim enough to pick up a hammer and not recognise the implicit violence of the implement in our hands.

### 13 - Jonah in my own private whale

*Entering the training compound I almost laugh at the double-decker beast I'm introduced to. Everything about it terrifies me!* Its size terrifies! Its smell terrifies! Its overwhelming colour terrifies! Reddest of reds! The colour of blood, of rage, of blind passion! Above all, its purpose terrifies! Surely I can't drive this!

'No!' it answers with a glint in its headlights – 'It is I who will drive you'. This is difficult to refute. Indeed, it is all too easy to see how the bus will carry me away. I will be a uniformed Jonah in an automotive whale.

But surely they're not expecting us to get in the bus on the first day!? – Wrong.

'Careful how you close the gate, it gives your fingers a nasty nip if you shut it too quickly!' advises my instructor. Immediately, I experience what he means.

'I did warn you!'

Indeed, the dislike between bus and driver - beast and man - is mutual: like a horse with a novice rider the bus doesn't see why it should let you sit on it, let alone take it for a spin: who the hell are you? Puny - petrified as you press the ignition button; pathetic as you push down the accelerator pedal with no power at all. Get off! Go back to your little life. This beast is for the big boys. And some of them are, as I say, big; in fact some are, to put it delicately, enormous bastards who look like they've been in training for the Obesity Olympics for the past four years. One or two have gold medal potential. Try as I might to blend in, I cannot help but feel like a different species.

Our instructor, a man who likes, sinisterly enough, to be called 'Big Len', is clearly a man of their same metal. Right on cue he puts us (them) at our (their) ease, remarking on his own and our (their) general bodily composition:

'You don't need me to tell you, this is a sedentary job; and for those of you who haven't swallowed a dictionary with your fry-up this morning, in plain English you will be sitting in a seat – all day every day. This is not a job where you will get any exercise. But then, as people go, I like to think we're built for comfort not for speed.'

All buses are automatic. So is your fear of every aspect of them. And like their gears, you progress fluently from anxiety to dread, from fear to panic when you sit in the seat for the first time. Big Len, the instructor hovers over you like the spirit of bad luck. You depress the accelerator pedal to get used to the sound of the engine revs: nothing happens. You press it harder. Still nothing.

'That's the brake, mate. You've got your foot on the brake.' Big Len's contempt is as routine as his boredom. He's seen it all – you all – a thousand times before. He knows you won't last, won't cut it: why should he care? He's here to put you through your paces, get you up and running ASAP, get you out of his hair so he can go home – but not by bus.

When you finally manage to put your foot on the right pedal of course the engine roars away.

'Hold on, hold on, Lewis! We're not on the front row of the grid!' He likes that one: the Formula One put-down: the glamorous image contrasts so perfectly with the bus's speedless banality.

'There, treat the bus like a woman: gently... there, now she'll do what you want.'

But of course! Right on time, like the number 10 bus to oblivion, the dismal sexual cliché makes its appearance: and how profoundly appropriate it is in this deeply smutty environment. What does he say to the woman trainees, I wonder? It isn't long, back in the canteen, before I find out.

∞

## 14 – The oldest profession in the world

Of course, as a 'city boy' I flattered myself it didn't define me - work, I mean. You've got to do something; and short of debating whether to take a job as an assassin, who seriously considers the moral status of what they do for a living? It's just not done: you get on with it, your day, I mean, without asking any difficult questions; well, any questions actually. Whatever you do, you do it *for a living*: that's the point: it has nothing to do with who you are and everything to do with money: you do it solely to earn money: like a prostitute.

You could say we wage-earners are all respectable whores: we surrender our bodily dignity, our labour for money, in a transaction which is thus, in its cost to our self-esteem – albeit unconsciously - as highly-charged as a sexual transaction in all but genitalia. You could say that in serving the corporation, the company – whatever, you prostitute your spirit during the week so that, just like the hooker, you can afford the lifestyle that defines the person you really are at weekends and on holiday. There's the 'you' at the desk, answering phones or writing silly reports and having silly ideas about how to 'grow' the company (what is it, a pot plant?) - sitting there, next to people towards whom you are, at best, mostly overtly indifferent, at worst, covertly hostile; and there's the 'you' at home or in the pub or club laughing with people with whom you refute the ridiculous reality to which you've all just subjected yourselves during the day; the big practical joke called 'work' you've all just pulled on each other.

Unquestionably, some jobs are sexier than others. Grand Prix driver. Supermodel. Movie star. US President – er, that's it. A bus driver is not sexy. Working – day-to-day working - in The City is not sexy - though it thinks it is. What's sexy is the money and, of course, the power it buys. Money *is* power. Sex and money: is there an older relationship?

In retrospect I can smile at the prudishness I displayed in the face of the breasts of the lap dancer Ronnie hired for the birthday I naively confessed to in the weeks that passed as I pondered my resignation. That trap was avoidable. Conversely, once sprung, the breasts weren't.

In The City – and without, as I say, dwelling overly on the tired old clichés - you pretty soon learn that an evening out with the boys means risking being dragged into what are touchingly referred to as compromising situations. Celebrations of deals, parties for any old reason usually end up in clubs. One must drink oneself stupid after all: it's only good manners. The West end is pock-marked by gentlemen's clubs where, needless to say, gentlemen are in short supply.

∞

## 15 - Canteen protocol

*There's only one woman on our beginner's course.* At the end of our first day, sitting two losers away along the canteen table, she has an attractive, if slightly asymmetrical, elfinesque face, dyed black hair and short, black nails which she has bitten down to the quick – such fastidious digital observation is a vice of mine: I always notice the state of people's nails immediately. But what is this disconcertingly feminine woman doing here?

I stare at her hair insensitively like an adolescent: why dyed-black, I wonder? Is she in mourning? Maybe she's a Goth – yes, a good-looking woman-Goth-bus driver in a silly uniform just about suits the chaotic diversity of our present cultural worldview. Then, horror of horrors: gawping at her, I fail to realise until too late that she's returning my gaze. Oh my god, she thinks I fancy her. Maybe I do, but that's not the point. What is the point? Searching clumsily for it, I give her a sort of bland smile to neutralise the tension – a 'we're-not-each-other's-type-dear-but-I-wish-you-the-best-of-British-luck' kind of a smile. She rightly dismisses this and smiles back to confirm that I am, indeed, her type. Indeed, seemingly uncontaminated by the corrosive self-doubt that has immobilised me throughout my life, she moves her chair next to me.

∞

## 16 – The sanctity of prostitutes

On the odd (very odd) evening out with Ronnie – and on a purely aesthetic, Toulouse Lautrec sort-of-a level, of course - I confess I found prostitutes fascinating. There's a hierarchy of involvement in the sex industry, and theirs charts a well-worn, indeed, Hogarthian route into the seedy citadel of eventual despair via self-contempt. Exotic dancers, strippers, lap-dancers, escort girls, hotel hookers, street walkers; all wander in and out of the City Boy's Point-Of-View. But even when they take centre stage in the clubs and hotel rooms – these remarkable women possess the power of absence. For creatures so naked they wear an invisibility cloak that clothes their souls and keeps them from lascivious, prying eyes. You can see it in *their* eyes – or rather you can't because though the lights may be proverbially on, it's clear that no-one is home. The women, themselves, are miles away. In this they are mistresses of a necessary self-deception – and thus deeply related to their clients.

I can spot them now all the time when I'm driving the bus. They always stand out from their context, whether the background be the foyers of expensive hotels, crowded pavements outside bars, clubs, or lowly station entrances: glamorous or cheaply tarty, call-girl or hooker, beautiful or plain, they know they're lost souls. They pretend to pretend. But they know they can't; not really. It's all gone too far: they've taken despair to its logical conclusion. There's a sort of stark dignity in that kind of perdition. It's silently crying out for a redemption, which it may one day therefore receive. Whereas us: we don't even know we're in any danger from our quid-pro-quo arrangement with the perverse god of the salaried income. We're happy with the banality of our bargain, the deal with our quotidian devil: the sacrifice of all our daylight hours to the monstrous Beelzebub of money.

It's all there in complacent black and white at the end of every month: our paycheques detail the monstrous calculation of loss: the compulsory contributions to our own demise, the sum of hope we forfeit on a yearly basis: the final tax code of the soul. Strange that we suffer ourselves to endure such a disproportionately unforgiving calendar whereby we allow ourselves so little time for our own identity in return for so much effort spent. You'd think we'd never been taught to add up. But then in my case, I wasn't. Though I can remember using an abacus at school: I loved those coloured beads: pushing them smoothly along the line, along the wire into each other. Although that wasn't the point of it apparently. That was maybe the very first time art and science, profit and loss clashed in my mind. My job in The City was the very last.

## 17 – Health and safety

*'So you've got a death-wish, too?' Goth bus-driving girl smiles at me.* I can think of no witty reply – actually I can think of no reply of any kind because the shock of the day's training has rendered me dumb.

'Learning to drive a bus? In London?' she spells it out for me. 'Were you not terrified when you got the job? I went into the bathroom and cried.' Donna has a vital spark behind her eyes. I like her immediately. She also has a strong, very attractive Irish brogue.

'You're Irish', I observe brilliantly.

She looks down at herself, genuinely shocked, 'Jeezus, so I am!' then, exchanging another smile for a look of concern, she leans across to me gravely, as if breaking bad news.

'Are you sure you should be here? Only you don't sound like a bus-driver. Something about your vowels.' She smiles again, the proverbial ice broken. In fact, everything about this girl is an ice-breaker: she has a directness that ploughs unfailingly through one's arctic Anglican reserve, as if brooking no obstruction to greater intimacy.

'That is, if you don't mind me saying!' she inquires – 'which I'm sure you don't!' she adds superfluously. By now I like her even more. It's another of my faults to like people too quickly: uncurbed it leads to friendship, which can prove fatal. Best to avoid liking people – best... but not easy with Donna.

Truth is I positively applaud her outspokenness in confirming my belief that I don't belong here. But then who does? Certainly not Donna, who sounds like she should be doing stand-up in a Belfast club. She lights up a cigarette. Almost immediately the health and safety hounds are upon her.

'You can't smoke in here, luv!'

Donna exhales a plume of contempt in the direction of her policeman, before stubbing out her cigarette. 'No? So just what can I do, sweetie?'

Big Len, our chauvinist instructor's disembodied voice chirps up from another table: 'I can think of one or two things.'

'But not without dribbling, eh, chief?' Having wielded her Celtic scalpel in the vague direction of our hapless instructor, Donna then looks around the room with a visible distaste for what she sees.

'Jesus, looking at this dump, prostitution's not such a dumb option.' She disappears briefly down a brief rabbit-hole of despondency, but quickly emerges again.

'So what crime did you commit?' Again, I look blank in response. 'To end up in this penal colony?'

'Ah well, it's a long story.'

'Oh ay, lost your job in The City, did you?'

'Yes – how --- '

'Had to be that - or an actor: got that look about you: self-assured - but riddled with self-doubt.' My smile broadens. Again, both the anomaly of Donna's psychological acumen and the mysterious coincidence of our temperaments fascinates me.

'I did used to be an actor actually! Well, trained as one,' I assure her.

'Didn't we all! "Jeez, nothin' better t'do - spose I'd better be a Hollywood star" sort-a-thing!'

I begin to wonder if this Irish Goth knows all about me: perhaps I might even venture to mention ---

'D'yer never wonder there's something more to life... than this, I mean?' she interjects, gazing with quiet desperation at the synthetic wasteland that surrounds us. 'I mean, not 'this'... any bloody place. Sometimes I think I've missed my vocation: should've been a nun. But all that black they wear. 'Brides of Christ', my arse: black widows more like – skulking about like spiders.

'But your hair is black,' I observe, thinking I'll try a bit of this speak-your-mind game, but immediately regretting it. 'I mean, you said you don't like black....'

'Didn't say I didn't like black; just wouldn't want to wrap myself up in a black bed-sheet every day.... Anyway, I *am* in mourning.'

'You don't sound like it!' Again, I immediately regret diving in.

'Do I not? Well, now that's good to know.... Well, see you around – good luck with the bus driving thing!'

With that, Donna rises and wanders off as purposefully as she arrived, no doubt to break ice somewhere else in South-East London's emotional arctic. And I wonder what she meant by being in mourning, and suddenly I think she is very difficult to read, this outspoken Irish woman who wears her heart on her sleeve. Perhaps her frankness is just another pose, perhaps the heart on her sleeve is a false one, hiding the real one somewhere much deeper down? Whatever the case, she is apparently a darker horse than me whom she found so easy to read. And I wonder 'why am I so transparent? Does everything about me scream who I am, disguise it as I may?' But so what if it does? After Auckland Avenue, I literally have nothing to hide any more. I hope my path crosses with Donna again soon. I like her. Who cares if she's hiding something. Why shouldn't she, in this shit-hole?

∞

## 18 – Descent

Ultimately, then, and in the full glare of Ronnie's contempt - I decided to resign. Once and for all. Finito. Basta!

The event in Auckland Avenue had proved decisive. What, then, *had* happened in that venerable street to confirm my resignatory vocation?

Auckland Avenue – such a commonplace name for so transcendent an event – at least for me. But perhaps not. Isn't Auckland on the other side of the world? Certainly, what happened to me in that faceless suburban street was antipodean to my character. It was the other side of my world. And it dumped me there in an instant; left me like a convict, transported (for the crime of my own banality) from some equable sovereign shore to somewhere infinitely more dangerous and exotic.

Not that I didn't try to escape its implications. After Auckland Avenue hadn't I stayed on at the bank and tried to remain the same? – I really had. But I'd gradually fallen apart. Over time I became like the half-knitted jersey my grandmother laid aside one afternoon, which, left on my own, my delighted childish fingers had slowly dishevelled. After Auckland Avenue all the threads of me had begun to come undone: I gradually unravelled.

You know what I mean – no doubt it's happened to you – just that your street has another name.

Then what should I say about Auckland Avenue and the cataclysmic change it wrought in my life? Perhaps nothing – insofar as nothing can be said that doesn't falsify the event to a certain vital extent; nothing that doesn't merely describe it, I mean; as if such a experience could be captured and paraded around in words... words which are the pathetic, undernourished prisoners of the rational mind....

I'm not being mysterious. I'm talking about the sort of experience that changes you for good; even though you might pretend – *try* desperately to pretend - for a while it hasn't; try to carry on as if nothing's happened – though in reality you know everything has....

### 19 - Snobs and yobs

*Donna's in trouble. Surprisingly, she and Big Len, the instructor, have not hit it off during training.*

'An official warning, can you believe it? For what? Telling him to fuck off with his patronising comments? Shoulda kept ma mouth shut. Always been my problem. Honesty's a bloody stupid policy, don't you think?'

'You could appeal.'

'Ha! I'll tell you one thing: he won't force me out. I can't stand bullies. My upbringing,' she confirms with palatably bitter irony.

Inevitably it comes out: I learn that Donna comes from the same dubious social stable as me, namely, from what used to be quaintly referred to, even as late as the 70s, as a 'broken home'.

'Arsehole though he was, mum was still amazed when dad left her for another woman! "I find you cold", he said to her. Don't think she ever got over that: the shock of being called cold by a bloke who beat her up. She never went out with another man. Can't say I blame her.'

I stare into my tea to escape the general condemnation of my sex.

'Listen to me, I sound like one of those fuckin' all-men-are-rapists harpies! I'm not. I like men. Really I do. Love the bastards. Even my dad. I traced him, you know.' Of course, I did not know; this, indeed, being one of the several thousand facts about Donna that I did not know.

'- To a backstreet in Leytonstone. He had another family. Totally unrepentant, of course. Even said he couldn't remember hitting me! Can you believe that? I stayed for a cup of tea, met my half sister: little ten year old. Seemed a nice kid. Didn't get to meet my half-brother. Then I left. Never saw him again. He died of a heart attack. I cried when I heard. Can you believe that..?' She takes out a cigarette, flicks it around a bit, then puts it back, adding 'Perhaps my mother was cold...'

Donna got up and left me with this sudden doubt about her mother, which perturbed me. Can we be so wrong about people? Could I be, about my own father? Even my mother?

∞

## 20 – 'A little of Dostoevsky does you good...'

No, the event in Auckland Avenue was a seismic event, its earthquake split the ground of my identity in two beneath my feet that day. And there was no warning, no advance tremors in my psychological Richter Scale. Usually, in events such as these, we're told there's a clear psychological warning that something serious is about to happen. An event such as Auckland Avenue's thus has two causes: great happiness or unhappiness; though as Tolstoy (not Dostoevsky) pointed out, the latter is much more imaginative and inventive than the former - there being hundreds of ways to be unhappy, whereas, conversely, everyone is happy in roughly the same way, etc.

The list of our unhappinesses? Barring all the obvious extremities of human experience: war, persecution, torture, starvation, natural disaster, etc, life stages a host of admittedly less major, but still catastrophic events: maybe your marriage is collapsing, or your teenage child goes seriously off the rails, or you or someone you love gets ill, discovers a lump that shouldn't be there; or maybe ill fortune begins on an even more banal note: maybe you embark on a mysterious, prophetic losing streak: maybe the old friend slowly, imperceptibly but undeniably turns out to be a flake, maybe you don't get that five grand back, maybe the project fades, and with it the smile on your wife/lover's/partner's face; maybe the brave punt you made on going it alone suddenly looks like the most dim-witted folly imaginable; then maybe the £200 roll of notes drops from the pocket you forgot had a hole in it, and miscalculation means that your one remaining un-maxed credit card gets kept by the restaurant you're in; or you can't afford all the shopping in your basket, and keep the queue behind you waiting as you have to leave some things with the check-out girl; or you get distracted at the gas station and go over the ten quid's worth you meant to buy, so have to leave them your mobile as surety that you'll come back; then you're driving home and the carton of stale chips you bought from the seedy fish shop falls from your lap; and on getting home you find you didn't get that shitty third-rate job you were relying on to pay the increased mortgage... you'll have to move, too late you find your wife's already been looking elsewhere.... By the time you leave the roulette table of worldly disappointments you've lost your wallet, cash, car, job, house, wife, kids – basically you lose the plot completely.

Conversely, as Tolstoy conceded, the house of cards can collapse as a result of happiness too, simply because good things then become the yardstick against which you measure the rest of your substandard experience, which, failing to come up the mark, finds itself condemned to the purgatory of general disquiet, coloured by the curse of disillusionment. Beware that August in the perfect villa in the sun! - that autumn weekend in Paris! - the friendship which geographical distance brought to an abrupt, unpremeditated end.... No, after romance comes the failed love affair, after the stroll down the Champs Elysée comes the pavement pratfall in Auckland Avenue...

## 21 – Clutch Control

*Clutch control: when to engage the gears, when to employ the power, when to have the guts to move forward in life, when to go!* Clutch control – without it you've got nothing. And nothing is what I've got.

'We can't even start on steering until we've got a sense of the bus's power, now can we?' asks Big Len rhetorically.

Even though there's no actual clutch, still, seated at the wheel of the training bus I am locked in a rictus of self-doubt: I can't employ my own emotional clutch properly, can't get a handle on how much power to bring in, how much to rev up the engine, how to proceed gently without suddenly lurching the bus into a Formula One race from the grid in my mind.

'Look, what yer gonna do is just sit here and go backwards and forwards for as long as it takes to get this

44

right!' assures Big Len with a scarcely restrained sense of menace. Then he leaves me to one of his assistant trainers and goes off to assess one of the other less emotionally-disabled trainees. I see from a distance it is Donna.

For the rest of the morning, I myself am to be seen going backwards and forwards in the automotive version of autism. Forwards... stop! Backwards... stop! Forwards.... Across the yard I see Donna in her bus describing neat parabolas with Big Len looking on. She looks up, smiles and gives me the finger. Bitch. I like her even more.

∞

## 22 – No U-turn

Some decisions you make, some directions you take, consciously or otherwise, cannot be reversed from. You have to carry on, take them to their logical conclusion.

That was what happened when the... event – happened to me; the event that stopped my life in its comfortable tracks; that took me from the lap-dance of luxury as a city-boy and eventually led me here to this seat, behind this wheel.

Of course, 'event' is a poor word for what happened to me that morning as I walked down innocently average Auckland Avenue in Crystal Palace to my singing lessons – any word would be poor. As for the singing lessons? Yes, I sing. Well, used to. In nightclubs, bars, small concert-halls – and also what used to be quaintly referred to as working-men's clubs – tough gigs some of them: people with their backs to you all night long, laughing over you, around you, at you, generally unimpressed by your impersonation of Orpheus. Some gaudy underworlds are not to be gainfully trespassed upon, some tarty Eurydices have no wish to be won back.

### 23 - Donna as the poetess, Sappho

*'Every day's a leap into the unknown really.' Donna looks distractedly out of the canteen window.* Or she would if there were one. In reality, there's just a small skylight, which she gazes up at.

'A lover's bloody leap. Kill or cure... at least that's what I tell my husband.... I told Clive to fuck off too, actually,' she observes as an afterthought to her more lyrical Sapphic reflections.

"Clever Clive" the depot manager, the same Mr Clive Grant who interviewed me, is, we soon learn, known by the soubriquet 'clever', on account of his appalling organisational skills. His office is apparently a punctiliously ordered chaos cluttered with contradictory, potentially lethal alterations in rotas, timetables and routes.

Then Donna explains mysteriously. 'He was giving me this sermon about respecting senior staff and I thought "this is ridiculous: I'm facing life and death at home and here's this shitty little man behind his big desk telling me I've got to calm down! I said "like to see you fucking calm down with what I'm facing!'

'What did he say?'

'He sacked me.'

'What!'

'No, I'm kidding. I went back with the union rep. We all sat down in a perfectly mature fashion: Clive, me and the union rep and agreed Big Len should, in effect, go and fock himself.'

Then, getting up from the table, having triumphed over my sex again, Donna offers her 'hail and farewell':

'Bob's your uncle: warning rescinded!' She smiled and was gone.

Donna's certainty about the avuncular identity of Bob – contradicted by the fact that my own father actually happens to be called Bob - set me thinking. Is anyone really who we think they are? Do we really know anyone? In revealing her doubts about her own father earlier, Donna had reinforced my own about mine. If only Bob had been my uncle - and not my father, it might all've been much simpler! Then again, perhaps Bob was my uncle and that was why I always felt so strange about him: he certainly behaved more like an uncle than a father. Had mother held another secret from me? What sort of a man was he: this Bob, my father? You tell me - apart from being a solicitor, I mean.

Looking back, I'm not sure there was anything to him apart from being a solicitor. He did everything by the book. Exactly which book, I never knew, but one full of precedents, a sort of 'colour-by-numbers' rule book for adults. Certainly, in the brief periods I spent with him as a child, I could never make him out. Conversely, I did learn that there were certain basic things wrong with me.

'I'm just going to the toilet, dad.'

'No you're not.'

'Pardon?'

'We don't say toilet in this house; we say lavatory – or loo for short. – And we don't say' pardon' either. We're not beggars – if we don't hear something, we say 'what?'

'What?' I asked my father.

' I said if we....' Then realising my childish joke he almost smiled.

Thus elocution lessons assumed pride of place in my brief, transient relationship with my father. Installed for a few summer weeks in his house, I learned to pick up the aitches I had been forced to drop on the council estate; learned to hold a knife and fork in a certain way, pronounce certain words specifically – 'gar–arge', rather than 'garridge'; learned not to say certain words at all: 'lounge', 'serviette' and 'couch', et cetera. Following this brief, intensive tuition in social etiquette, I was then dumped by said dad back into the arena of the council estate, where being found in possession of an 'aitch' was deemed sufficient cause for several remedial beatings until I learned to drop said aitches again. Thus it was that I learned that class identity, nay human nature itself, could only truly be defined by vowels, nouns, cutlery and holiday destinations!

So basic to us is this classifying compulsion that one can well believe Kant's insight about time and space: that they themselves represent a primal form of classification, and as such are not external to our perception, but part of the structure of perception itself. Time and space are not outside but inside us: like tools we use in order to perceive our world, to classify it and put it in order. And, unfashionable as it sounds, we do need to bestow order. Just to perceive things, to open your eyes, to smell, feel, taste, touch and hear is to come into contact with a chaos of sensations, a world that one desperately needs to make sense of; the same is true of people. One perceives fellow souls whose qualities - or lack of them - one must assess in order to ascertain whether or not they present any threat or promise of reward to, and for, oneself. This is a crassly Darwinian over-simplification admittedly – but as such all the more accurately mirrors the subject it analyses, inasmuch as class itself is a necessarily crass over-simplification of human nature. The point is that classifying people and things is inevitable and useful, so long as we beware the criteria upon which we base our classifications.

Anyway, the lecture's over – and so is our tea-break. Suddenly my stomach is playing up again: this has started to happen over the past week or so, a month into training. Somehow, without calling attention to my sense of urgency, I must run to the loo.

∞

## 24 – Why sing?

So there I was, humming away with my headphones on, improvising to a Frank Zappa song in Auckland Avenue. I remember a couple of teenage girls passing me by with barely restrained laughter. Kate always says I sing flat with my headphones on. This is rubbish, of course – though apparently the girls agreed with her. But then it is never a good idea to sing in public. Happiness is provocative: it invites retaliation.

Now I think of it: why *did* I sing - in public – professionally, I mean? I regard myself as a private person. And yet there I was, seeking to make money from my happiness, to profit from my distress. After all, nobody sings unless they're happy or sad. Singing is thus an extraordinary act, a bizarre expression of emotional extremes; and the fact that we *enjoy* singing is an equally bizarre confession of our *need for* those same emotional extremes; an admission that emotional extremes are, in fact, where we feel most at home. For only emotional extremes breed music – without them there would be no song. And, in fact, there isn't – most of the time. Most of the time we don't sing. In fact, it's normal *not to sing*.

We addicts of emotional ecstasy! How early on in life do we learn to be ashamed of our own exaltation and despair? No, singing is not for general display in front of those who would set our deepest feelings at nought. Yet though we ourselves may lose our talent for song – still we remain addicted to it – and addicted to those in whom the instinct has not died. Is this one of the reasons why we love singers and actors? They heroically reclaim our identity as creatures capable of intense emotion; reaffirm our capacity for utter transport? Is this why even Karaoke exerts a morbid fascination?

How Ronnie had loved his Karaoke! Such was the power of his self-belief that he bestowed his gift on you too – whether you liked it or not. Back in the day 'Summer Breeze' was Ronnie's show-stopper:

"When I come home, from a hard day's work, see you waiting there, not a care in the wooorrrrrrld!" Ronnie would howl, drunkenly focussing on some unsuspecting woman in the bar whilst drowning in his own private vat of Afro-American glamour. The Isley Brothers would've been proud.

"Aaah summmer! Summer breeze!" confirmed Ronnie, as the rest of us died laughing. Jetted by private rapture back to Ohio, Ronnie was in 70s heaven. All that was missing was the 'Afro' – and the talent....

Ronnie.... One didn't know whether to laugh or cry. So one did both, confounded by Ronnie's admirable lack of self-knowledge. He was happy after all.

But why did I sing? Me, Matt Grant, singer.... And why was I singing that morning in Auckland Avenue? Did something in me know what lay just around the corner?

## 25 – Turning circle

*Locked in the bus with Big Len, the instructor, I realise that claustrophobia is not just physical; you can feel claustrophobic in someone else's presence, the rigid confines of whose personality enclose you in a terrifyingly small space, starving you of breath and vision.* In this way, people can sentence you to imprisonment with their view of you, of the world. Such a man is Big Len. It is not the mingling of his cheap aftershave and stale breath that constrict me; rather it is the fact that here is a fellow-convict in the prison of circumstance in whom I cannot confide one iota of angst, since he refuses even to realise he's in gaol; indeed, he loves serving a life sentence. Today, not wholly without irony, he is teaching me how to go round in circles.

'You see those traffic cones up ahead? They're not traffic cones, are they?' – Big Len is evidently a great fan of the rhetorical question.

'Aren't they?'

'No, they're not; they're people; in fact it's a bus stop full of people queuing for the bus behind you!

'Don't start turning left-hand down until your bus is at least half way past it, otherwise you'll hit the cones and when you hit the cones you won't just be knocking down cones, will you?'

No, I will be knocking down a bus queue; we get the point, which is not to say we can manoeuvre the bus equally easily.

There is an act of faith in driving a bus, an unconscious investment of belief in the laws of physics, the truths of mathematical geometry. It's not that, as you go left hand down at a T-junction, you think 'the square on the hypotenuse is equal to the sum of the squares on the other two sides; it's more that the intuitive genius of your physicality spot-checks the distances, angles and shapes involved in a corner and then calculates the equation, instantly and mysteriously coming up with the right answer so that the bus turns correctly without killing a bus queue – or not, as the case may be.

'There now, the back end of your bus has just clipped three cones and what've you done? You've killed fifteen people, haven't you?'

I have.

'And how do you feel about that?'

Surprisingly OK actually. As I see the cone-people sprawling fatally injured across the tarmac I realise how disconnected I am with my current circumstance. And those cone-people probably had it coming anyway; who knows what they got up to in their private lives? No, two or three cone-people more or less will not adversely affect the progress of our beleaguered species. Then the instructor's voice breaks back into my Hitlerian worldview.

'I'll tell you how you feel: you feel devastated. You go home but you cannot sleep; they tell you it was just an accident but you cannot forgive yourself.

'One small mistake, one small error of judgement and you've not only killed fifteen people at a bus-stop you've affected the lives of all their relations – all those children you've left parentless; all those mums and dads whose kids you've just run over: for that you will never be able to forgive yourself, will you?'

No, I will not. I suddenly have a profound respect for cone-people the world over; these little orange-skinned, pointy-headed souls who have revealed my closet racism I now embrace with a contrition and compunction worthy of an eremite experiencing an epiphany.

'This is what driving a bus is all about!' sermonizes the instructor.

'You're not just delivering people to their destinations, you're their guardian, the custodian of their safety. Whilst they're on board your bus you are responsible for their lives – or deaths!'

Suddenly I see that I am no longer a trainee bus-driver learning how to transport passengers from A to B, but a Charon ferrying the souls of the dead to their appropriate destinations in the underworld of circumstance.

No way did it state this on the job spec. At no point did I see the requirement 'Must be prepared to assume the mythical proportions of a minor classical icon serving a major pagan god...'

The body is deeply mysterious: it shares intimate connections with the mind – no doubt even is the mind - but in material form.... Anyway, the fact is that over the first few weeks of driver training my body adapts to the bus's monstrous new proportions and perspectives; strangely, inexplicably my body begins to adopt the larger turning circle life has suddenly demanded of it. As if by magic I stop murdering cone-people at bus-stops; concomitantly, their relations cease to blame me: at night in dreams I no longer have to explain to grieving cone-mums and cone-dads how a moment of over-steering madness has taken their little cone-lings from them forever. I approach the T-junctions of life with a new-found expertise: I believe in my body's geometrical acumen: it is a prophet in the laws of maths and physics whose linear prognostications I gradually learn to trust implicitly. I am indeed Charon: in my mind I do indeed suavely steer the souls of unsuspecting passengers to peaceful destinations.

Actually, learning to steer the bus in training at the depot, it strikes me that human personality has a turning circle as large as a double-decker bus; this is why you need other people to give you a certain amount of space in life. Our vices and virtues are unwieldy and to avoid collisions we must obey a psychological highway code every bit as pedantic as the actual one that confronts me on my driver training course. This highway code is, in fact, what we call 'morality': that little book of rules and regulations that enable us to manoeuvre round each other reasonably efficiently without killing ourselves or others in the process of travelling the A to B map of our desires.

Friendships thus constitute the various qualities of roads on which we travel: some, you don't need transport for; in fact you delight in dispensing with mechanics of any kind insofar as the friendship is the destination and there is thus nowhere to travel to. Such friendships are as easy and amiable as Parisian boulevards: you link arms and time disappears in an intoxicating haze of stylish conversation and perfumed emotions. Other friendships may, of course, be tight and twisting mountain passes, ironically full of impasses and fraught with negotiations; still others are quiet country lanes where nothing much is achieved and hours pass in a wholly personable pastoral kind of a way, though they leave you longing for the city at the end of the day; still others are just dead ends: you try and find a way out of them, but left or right you just end up having to turn around and admit defeat.

If my metaphors trespass on a certain triteness here it is because I am trying to make sense of the circumstance that appears to have forced me to learn to drive a double-decker bus – and I have found, predictably enough, that transport metaphors come in handy. They bring our imaginative journey in line with the physical one by revealing their shared elements. When, for example, a lover says to you: 'I need time, a bit of space', they are being both literal and metaphorical. What sort of space do they need? Answer: one that doesn't have you in it; one that is, however, large or small, thus both materially and psychologically liberating; delivering them, as it does, of your presence in any way, shape or form.

Yes, we are all practised in the art of turning circles.

∞

## 26 – Actors as professional liars

But then nothing could've prepared me for what happened in Auckland Avenue – for its assault on my personality – even though my experience as an actor had introduced me to the idea that personality itself can be a movable feast, so to speak. Drama school had taught me that you – or who you think you are - is not always such an easy thing to pin down; that personal identity is not the assured entity it appears to be. Sure, when you act a part, you're pretending; doesn't matter how artful the pretence is, or how whole-heartedly you embrace it using 'The Method' - ultimately, acting is still artful dissemblance: you're not really Macbeth seeing a dagger before you. Or are you? Certainly, some actors do get dangerously close to the parts they play: you hear them say they can't shake them off after work; that they actually become the people they play – at least for a while until the roles wear off. But if we can forget ourselves and become someone else, what does this say about the provisional nature or our 'selves'?

Of course, to a certain extent, we're all actors. And, of course, we are not limited to just two personae; we might have three or four or however many we need to get us through the day: the devoted family man or woman, the diligent manager, dutiful son or daughter, slouch, slattern or slob, the liar and lothario, lecher, puritan or prig, the virgin, adulteress or slut, 'and all stations in between', so to speak. We call on all of these, put on the masks as and when they suit us – apparently undisturbed at their inherent lack of consistency; at the implication that there might in fact *be no* consistency of personality in our lives; that we might in fact be all these different persona. And if we are – then who – or what - really are we?

## 27 – A trial with Manchester United

*It turns out that Donna is both happily and unhappily married; happy with two wonderful kids; not so delighted by the fact that her husband has recently been diagnosed with Parkinson's.* I tentatively ask after him.

'Not so good this week, thanks. I can't bear seeing him struggle: it hurts, it makes me...' she weeps silently. 'Paul is – was so... active. Loved his football. Fucking game. United looked at him when he was a kid; he still trains with... used to train....'

Not that it matters anymore, she adds. No, it doesn't, not any more, when Paul can hardly hold a teacup straight, let alone waltz pass three defenders with a ball....

Life strikes us down – indiscriminately, accidentally, meaninglessly, ruthlessly. Life is a wrecking ball left on, unmanned upon the architecture of the soul. Life takes your breath and legs away, cripples young men like Paul to whom it suddenly gives Parkinson's....

So that's why Donna is in mourning. The man she loves is probably going to die, slowly, dismally, and painfully. Yes, 'they' may develop a drug to cure it; they may not. So, as it is, she is stoically driving a bus to make up the shortfall in what were once joint salaries. Her kids are with her mother during the day. Not ideal but what can you do? Offering no answer, the god of fate smiles wickedly and turns away. That is, if you believe in him. Personally, I have my doubts about the bugger. If pressed, I have to confess that I believe life is, for the most part, an utter lottery – and not one that ends up in the south of France for one person in 14 million; no, once you've elected to come back, to be reborn in this realm of human being, pretty much anything can happen to you – and usually does. As for happiness - that ludicrous country bumpkin of a word! - its attainment seems to depend on the most fragile contingencies of circumstance. In good moods I prefer to believe in my own moment-by-moment aspiration as the agency of my contentment. As that effervescent optimist Walt Whitman declares (no doubt I misquote) 'henceforth I ask not good fortune, henceforth I myself <u>am</u> good fortune....' – What? Even as a bus driver?

∞

## 28 – The Fluidity of Personality

What I'm getting at about personality – in regard to what happened to mine in Auckland Avenue - is that it is in fact, a lot more fluid than we like to think. At least it was in my case that morning as I walked, as I say, to my singing lessons...

Actually, in attempting to address the 'event' (which, I apologetically concede, is a coy word), 'fluid' is a highly relevant word. The body is, as we know, ninety-something per cent water; we're born via our mother's amniotic waters, having slept for nine months in the depths of that same, warm, calm ocean; then we start to drink fluids from our mother's breast; giving that up, we replace it with the saccharine drinks of childhood, the sugared, iridescent waters of innocence; moving swiftly on into adolescence we then begin to experiment with other intoxicating waters, simultaneously bitter-sweet, steeped in the mystery of fermentation. The rites of passage of teenage drunkenness then grant us access to an adult lifetime of fermented escape from the banal measurements of the rational, from the carceral confinement of personality.

## 29 – Life as a 'hill-start'

*The fear of the hill-start is in our DNA - and it stands between me and training success: just this one last hurdle before the test: perfect a competent hill-start. Because we cannot afford to roll back in a bus.*

In fact, rolling backwards out of control, unable to carry on, to proceed, progress when life gets difficult is, you could say, the opposite of life. and standing still is no good either. A village idiot can stand still on one leg. No, I must prove myself to Big Len by my ability to move this bus forward, to show the fat bastard I can progress on my own two legs, under my own steam. In this scenario, Big Len is a surrogate father. And how proud our parents are when we take our first steps! When the stabilisers come off the bicycle!

So here I am at the top end of Duppas Lane where it meets Croydon Old Town Road. I've brought the bus to a satisfactory halt and, full of a sense of achievement, here I sit. The way is clear both ways, I ready myself to begin the slight incline; get ready to engage drive... but mistakenly disengage the semi-automatic handbrake first - and rolled back... and back... and back – and then back some more.

'Handbrake! Put your fuckin' handbrake back on!' Big Len's urgent command distantly penetrates my silent realm of mute terror as I feel the stream of backwardness flow in my veins. Big Len has an override brake pedal, but he refuses to use it in order to prove a point. Will we then roll backwards all the way down the hill, all the three miles back to the depot, hitting rows of victims on the way? Or just keep rolling downhill for eternity?

'Use yer fuckin' handbrake!'

An arm reaches down. The god of handbrakes intervenes and the bus stops just short of the gates of hell.

'What the fuck were you doin'!?' inquires Big Len.

What indeed. I explain that I'd gone blank for a moment.

'Yeah, well goin' blank kills people, so if I was you I'd stop goin' blank as quickly as you fuckin' can - know what I mean?'

Cone-people again. Did I squash any of them? No, no-one behind me – a fact Big Len had secretly known all along as he left me to panic. He takes a deep breath.

'Now – excuse my French, but that is exactly what happens when someone panics! OK?'... OK.

'Now you're not gonna panic again, are you? This is a simple fuckin' hill-start - 'scuse my French again - and you're gonna do it the way you've done it a million times at the depot. Right?'

Right. And I do.

What is it about panic? Why do we panic? Who is the god of panic?

Ah.... Pan. Pan - mischievous magician of an alternative reality more real than our own!

∞

## 30 - The necessity for drunkenness

Yes, looking back, I was dead drunk in Auckland Avenue; though not any drug, drink or chemical that you can buy or get prescribed.

Ah drunkenness – vulgar practise of the British! Subtle art of the world! Who can do without its ecstasy and bizarre clarity in some shape or form? Drunkenness – which is nothing but an empowering escape from the impotence of one's quotidian personality. Drunkenness - that state of mind in which everything suddenly becomes intensely alive! Why would we need altered states if our natural state sufficed? No, life needs an additive. The drugs *do* work. They must. Who, in their right mind would eschew their vital revelation? Of course, there are drugs – and drugs.... The alcoholic pursues his drunken vision via the bottom of a glass; the meditator his intoxicated rapture through communion with the divine; the lover her tongue-touching euphoria in lubricious unity with the beloved; whilst for those who prefer a gentler, though scarcely less ecstatic exaltation, the inspirations of music, poetry and art hold up their rainbow champagne glasses!

No, the only problem with drunkenness is that it too frequently eludes us! Conversely, of course, it can visit itself upon you utterly unplanned, with no drink, no lover, no meditation and no art; indeed, no effort at all of any kind whatsoever. Such was the hallucinogen of Auckland Avenue.

First, let me just say that LSD is a drug I've never taken. Afraid of its vaunted capacity to alter the very structure of my mind, to radically re-organise the nature of perceptions at an irreversibly deep level; and also deeply aware of my own sensibility's already highly sensitised volatility, I refrained whenever I had the chance – and I had many – to indulge in Lysergic Acid Diethylamide. Throughout my teens, at college, at drama school, then later in the city, never a tab passed my lips. I needn't've worried: so-called 'normal' life gave me the same trip that morning anyway.

### 31 – Never relax

*I stare straight ahead. As advanced trainees, we're now out on the road every day, having graduated to busier streets – still passengerless of course, apart from Big Len.*

'Never relax – not for a moment! The moment you relax is the moment you crash the bus!' reassures Big Len.

No, I stare straight ahead... at the road – and life itself. I can now drive this big red bastard. Even the bus begrudgingly agrees. Its power seems to simmer with repressed rage under my hands.

And I too am become a strange beast: reconciled to my creature discomforts, there is never a moment in all this when I don't accept it; profoundly accept it and deeply rebel against it at the same time. I've got to feed my family: that's not an option; it does not represent one of your average Westerner's dire, potentially life-changing dilemmas, like, say, having to choose between going to the movies on Friday or Saturday; eating at this Chinese restaurant or that Pizzeria. You've got to live, got to put food on the table. Poverty is not metaphorical. It's a literal truth. We live life first and foremost in the actual; only when we've succeeded in fulfilling basic functional needs can we move onto the abstract. Yes, artists often suffer, but art itself is still the luxury of the metaphorically well-heeled, those lucky enough to go comparatively decently shod through life. Even Van Gogh had a little yellow house in the South of France....

So the sense of necessity in what I'm doing does provide a kind of dumb, depressed reconciliation, even a certain gloomy peace of mind at times. Poverty drove me mad in a short space of time; now circumstance has taken the wheel and driven me to drive a bus, so I might as well learn how to do it. Two weeks til the final exam. Hold very tight please. Ding! Ding!

∞

## 32 – The Event in Auckland Avenue

This will sound crazy. At least I hope so...

Put simply: as I headed from the station down Auckland Avenue towards my singing lesson that morning (listening, somehow appropriately, as I say, to Frank Zappa's 'Inca Roads' on the headphones) I walked inadvertently through a doorway. Not just any door, no - the most important door I would ever walk through in my life. And it was not a door I had any choice but to walk through – because the door was everywhere I looked.

Doorways are crucial and beautiful: they frame the present; without them we could not proceed from one place to another, from one state of mind to another. As such, doorways have measurements drawn to the scale of past, present and future. This particular door was bound by no such proportions. Not made of wood or stone; indeed, with no height or width at all – possessing only, you could say, infinite depth. I would call it a 'portal' but this is not Sci-fi. In a way, it was the door that opened into *me*, with the effect that everything suddenly saw *me* – and saw that there was, well, no-one there to see.

That morning in profoundly ordinary Crystal Palace, a propos of nothing and no-one, without prior hint or warning, I suddenly – and momentously – lost my grip on life: lost all touch with the thing that we unknowingly cling onto – *that deceptively intangible thing called personality*. You could say I suddenly died. And not in a manner of speaking.

Remember when you *were* a kid and you suddenly looked round in the street to find mummy nowhere near? The terrifying rush of aloneness! That's it! - except replace that terror with a tidal wave of emotional release... an atomic fusion of relief, of simultaneous, celestially light-hearted, oceanically deep peace.

### 33 - The tyranny of the diary

*Training is over! The day of my driving test draws suddenly, horribly near – under a week away.*

Like lies we've told, or words we regret; like actions that come back to haunt us, those dark diary dates we've been hiding from always and inexorably come round: the day we've been dreading dawns. Dentists, doctors, driving tests – you signed up for them with a bravado born of distance; but now here, with a heavy ghoulish step and their own hot breath, they stand and breathe in your fear...

I think about backing out, but I can find no pretext for doing so the shame of which doesn't prick even my hyper-insensitivity where public opinion is concerned. Of course, it's my wife's, Kate's, scorn and despair my conscience couldn't bear. Her good esteem is the measure of who I am.

No I will have to go through with it; will have to surrender to linear time reeling me in day by day, hour by hour: I am the dying fish upon its line....

One is drawn to wonder why one always swallows the bait? What attracts us to the smell of the diary-date? Why are we drawn to make any dates in the first place? Why make plans beyond the morrow? Sufficient unto the day is the evil diary-date thereof, et cetera, et cetera. So why not just live a life which incurs no thought for the future; an eternal present tense requiring no insurance policy of consolatory events? You want to see a friend? See them now. If they can't see you now, then dare the possibility that you will never see them again. Why must we piece out our time? Why draw out a chain of links that ultimately confines us in a prison of diary-date proportions? Answer? Spiritual agoraphobia - a fear of the infinitely open spaces of the heart, the pitiless sun of loneliness from which we need a place to hide.

Diaries, calendars and wall-planners are, thus, welcome prisons; their days and weeks and monthly maps are paper-thin exclusions of eternity, a direct view of which would crush us with its gravity, annul our size and scale, our picture-frame proportion; reduce to dust our genteel prisons of curtain-neat security. By necessity, it appears we live in miniature, our wall-planners an act of self-defence against all-pervasive solitude whose sun would, as I say, blind us with its clarity.

So I set the digital alarm in my I-phone diary: for now my exam day remains red-ringed for next Thursday – The day of Thor – god of thunder, lightning and storms....

∞

## 34 – Phenomenal phenomena

So there I am – or suddenly *am not* – in Auckland Avenue, so to speak. All sense of self detonated like a child's lie revealed by a parent's piercing stare.

What *is* there instead of 'me' is... a burning spectrum of colour. Green trees bleed into blue sky! Lilacs fume with purple smoke! Neon traffic lights ignite in firework sparks of red, orange and green. – And cars! Cars are waves of movement! Their passing swells a tidal current of air that crashes into buildings and relapses; and as their automotive sea-surf sound collapses, an ocean of forms melt into one another. The colour spectrum has ignited. I am inside a rainbow, drowning in a liquid fire of perceptions.

Cast overboard, with the anchor of personality suddenly withdrawn, no longer moored to myself, I am both a cork adrift upon a sea and the current of sensations that flow into me: I am the ebb and flow of air I breathe, the pulmonary thrill of lungs emptied and filled, like a coastal inlet crashed by waves. Suddenly everything is in reach. Nothing escapes the purview of my rapture.

Take the sun. No, I mean – literally - 'take the sun'. I did. I had no choice.

What else was I to do? What with it being so ludicrously close to hand and all! If I hadn't reached up and taken it someone else would have done, and then where would we have been? In the dark. Or down at the front desk of the local nick, reporting the robbery of the sun from the sky to some cynically incredulous police sergeant with his finger itching on the trigger of a phone call to the men in white coats.

No, better that someone with at least some communal sense took the sun and looked after it. And in Auckland Avenue I was rich in communality. Indeed, in a not unprosaic sense, I *was,* momentarily, at least, the soul of communality. I partook of the nature of things. I *was* the nature of things. Ah but how the letter of the law kills....

I'll say this: I can report back that the arm of a man is combustible. But not in a bad way. In Auckland Avenue, as something we call an arm appeared to reach up to the sun and stroke its petals of flame, 'my' limb caught fire and I gently waved it up and down like a torch. I recall saying 'this is interesting, let's take this further'. So I put the sun down – well, put it back up on its shelf actually, because, like a child in a toy shop, my interest in the sun was almost immediately superseded by the branch of the tree on which I had momentarily set it down.

The delightful trouble was, the branch stopped being a shelf and reached out its arm to me, an arm of impossibly resolute elegance and power. Trees are not trees, they are sculptures holding a pose for an artist. Was I, then, the artist? Or was I the branch? Or both? Or neither?

## 35 – The wrong bin

*It's the day of my test and I'm in the canteen awaiting my time slot. Life has never felt so unreal.* Indeed, the bus depot is a hallucinogen that distorts those who breathe in its atmosphere, turning them into bus drivers. The trainees wish each other good luck.

Most humans are basically a decent bunch: they will try and give each other an even break if they can afford to. Not Phil the depot janitor. Phil has his sharp eye out for the small mistakes of life – the errors that condemn one to a purgatory of mutual dislike.

'You just put that cup in the wrong bin!'

I turn round and look at him just as I'm leaving the canteen to go to the loo before the test.

'I said you've just put that cup in the wrong bin - that's for stationary – paper, bills, receipts excetra - not plastic cups. Now you've made it all wet!'

I loathe it when people say 'excetra' - didn't Phil study any Latin ferfuxake! I sneer rhetorically in a moment of superb snobbish impotence.

'There wasn't any tea left in it,' I protest.

'So you say. I saw it spill out.'

'What?'

'I saw liquid spill out over the stationary bin. Now you'll have to fish it out.'

'Fish what out?'

'The cup! And change the bin liner. I've told Clive I ain't changin' no more soiled bins. It's been agreed! The people what make the mistake 'ave ter put it right. You've made the mistake., You'll 'ave to do it – or be reported – up to you....'

"Are you joking?' I ask Phil seriously. But, of course, he's not.

'Oh for chrissake! Here you are then.' I grapple with said bin.

'Old bin liners go round the corner!' Phil confirms.

I haul the plastic caul out of its container, march aggressively round the corner and fling it with the others. Re-appearing, I wipe my hands in Phil's direction – but he's gone.

And I wonder how Phil the janitor came to be like this. So set in his ways, intransigent beyond the call of duty, Phil is an SS war hero of pettiness – a Nazi commandant collating the ultra-pusillanimous forces of order, driving the rest of us mad. But how did he get like this? Who gave him the uniform emotions? His mother and father no doubt. Is it just an accident of parentage that makes a 'Phil the fascist janitor'?

This accident of life! Certainly of birth! Who chooses their parents, or the circumstances their parents wrestle with as they try to slot you, their hapless progeny, more or less clumsily into the diaries of their doubtful fates?

No, by hook and crook, more by luck than judgement each of us has fallen back into the dubious lap of life through a mother's womb, the dark cave we make our way out of at birth. Subsequently, fate demands that we rise from the ape-like dependency of babyhood back up into the angelic psychological posture for which our human capacity for evolution predestines us. - Or ought to.

My point is that adult life is essentially a neoplatonic cock-up, and if we are eventually to return to Plotinus's union with the original carefree ecstasy of The One, then most of us realise we might as well give each other a leg up. I say 'most' – not, apparently Phil or all the other old lags in the depot who do not share my neoplatonic sympathies: hard-bitten pros whose sense of bitterness long ago precluded any sight or sound of heaven. Age, simple age can be a corrosive: it eats into the hidden sub-structure of the soul just as voraciously as rust into the sills of a double-decker bus. And the decomposition of metal and flesh proceeds in remarkably similar stages. Thus happiness rusts.... (Ten minutes to go 'til my test.)

∞

## 36 – Joyfully defying rational description

Of course, the trees came alive in Auckland Avenue – why would they not? For trees are locked in our view of them - stuck in the adhesive of time we immerse them in. By falling in love with trees one liberates them, dissolves their movement from the stasis of our stare. Then they dance. They hold out their arms to waltz with us. As lovers we cannot refuse. And so, without moving, I danced with the trees in Auckland Avenue. And as I did so, everything else came close to watch. And inasmuch as an audience is consummately involved with the genius of a work of art through their absorption in it; so in Auckland Avenue nothing was excluded. Auckland Avenue was life in its totality – a globe with no polar opposites, no 'you' 'I' and 'it'; only a dynamic current washing the shores of a perceptual world! A world in which you no longer smell the perfume of the flower, you *are* the flower's scent, the taste of apple in your mouth....

Ah, Planet Earth may be the only name we have for our madly spinning globe – but it is deceptive nonetheless, for the earth is weightless. How easily I bore the gravity of my own footsteps! How lightly the cohesive burden of my own earth! Moonwalker in my own weightless boots!

What did I think was happening? I *didn't...* - 'think', I mean. In Auckland Avenue, thought, itself, disappeared into a vortex, and with it, time; time slipped and slid off the sundial of consciousness like the melting hands of

Dali's surrealist clocks. Time ceased to measure anything! Time which is, perhaps, only a compass point upon a map to draw up notions of separation between past, present and projected selves. But if you are joined to everything, then there is no time.

No, in Auckland Avenue, time slowed down and stopped completely – and then began to drift aimlessly... the points on time's clock become dandelion seeds in the breeze. You can blow the hours this way or that. Moments of time are seeds on the breath of a child...

## 37 – The test

*This is it: the moment arrives. I sink myself into the seat of the bus.* My biggest fear is that I will pass this test and thus pass through the door into a life I have nothing but barely concealed contempt for: the world of the rigid timetable, the unbending schedule and routine, the foetid cabin.

My examiner is a nice old guy. I feign a certain degree of nervousness to get him on my side.

I start off well enough, no sudden movements, no excessive braking or accelerating. I come to several halts easily and start off again fluently without alarm. My indicators are all well-timed and all the indications are that the wicked god of success is winking at me.

Then, approaching traffic lights, I get into a hopelessly wrong inside lane - a furious stream of cars surging past me, preventing my access to the right filter, which is suddenly a conundrum – both as near and far way as France seen from Dover on a clear day.

Sadly – weirdly – I don't panic. I let the traffic file in front of me and wait endlessly for some kind soul to let me in. The sweet old lady in the Nissan Micra, who I stereotypically expect to take on that identity only scowls as I begin to make my move: she pokes her minnow forward edging out my whale. Disguising my exasperation, feeling the examiner's eyes on me (they sit across the aisle in the disabled seats), I merely use the occasion to exercise the easy patience of the saint I have become.

Typically, subverting prejudice, it's a young bloke in a white BM who lets me in. I cross in front of him with a kingly hand signal of measured gratitude and dock into my rightful lane. I then turn right – slowly, smoothly, eternally right – into the clearly marked avenue of success - and ultimately that same terrifying life of routine, uniform haplessness....

'Well, I'm pleased to tell you you've passed, Mr Grant.' The smile I return the examiner is so piss-poor it immediately betrays my profound dismay. 'I did say "passed"', he jokes as I sit reduced by my spurious success to utter silence.

Yes, there were one or two points to watch out for – aren't there always? Lane discipline, of course, and my mirror work was at times a little cursory, he burbles on; my attention frequently wavered between looking forward and behind – an error unquestionably reflecting my dread, I want to explain to him, of the future I was carving out, contrasted with my desire desperately to retrace my steps back into the recent past. – But the truth is unavoidable: I have passed.

Mirror, signal, manoeuvre...

I get home and turn left into the bathroom.

Mirror, signal, manoeuvre.

I reach out for the hot water tap, soap and razor.

Mirror, signal, manoeuvre.

Wash, dry off, and go to bed.

Mirror, signal, manoeuvre.

My unconscious drives me into dreams I don't remember.

Mirror, signal, manoeuvre.

At dawn I wake up: Kafka's nightmare has come true:

Mirror, single, manoeuvre.

Overnight I have turned into a bus driver.

Mirror, signal, manoeuvre.

I get ready to beetle off to work on my eight new chitin legs.

∞

## 38 – Slow-mo....

Yes, time, too, is a dance. In Auckland Avenue it waltzed from its usual fast-forward into slow-mo.

What is it about slow-mo? Why do the seeds of the dandelion clock transfix us so? Is it the possibility visibly offered to us to live life set in a different key, at a different rhythm? Or is it that slow-mo allows us to see what is actually happening to us *all the time* slowed down *in time? To see ourselves in detail with the luxury of slow-motion?* If so, why aren't we born into a life of slow-motion? Why has the speed been hurried up – actually, coarsened - to 24 frames per second? Was god just a primitive technician, a clumsy inventor? Are we the Daguerreotype of his soul? Did God make a lousy camera and force us to live with a third-rate blurred image of ourselves?

It's like the moment glass shatters: you never normally see that split second when you break a window: only, in the case of the event in Auckland Avenue you do – in fact, that's all you see: the beauty of breaking glass;

life as a flow of forms breaking down and changing into each other; life as a kaleidoscope - life as breaking glass in slow motion.

## 39 – The un-sanctity of marriage

*A deadly silence hangs like a pall over the breakfast table the morning following my bus driving test success.* Kate doesn't know whether to laugh or cry, what to say or why. She pretends not to see my uniform slung across the back of the chair.

I sense in her silence a certain repressed resentment at my distress – and why not? There's nothing worse than a moaner. Either do it, or don't do it; but don't sit there crying into your cornflakes, waiting for mummy to make it better. Because mummy's got her own problems: caring for your infant son whilst working part-time herself – remember?

Yes, I remember.

I remember lots of things. I remember you and me making love in the afternoon, or driving down to the sea in the evening on a whim; or hopping over the Channel to wander down the sylvan lanes of soft Montmartre, or on the plains of the sombre Somme to wonder at the war graves... (Incidentally, is it not deeply revealing of the god of music, Apollo's sadistic irony that a place, formerly of such deafeningly hellish misery, should now resound with such perversely peaceful silence? Of course, it's the dead that exude the unearthly silence. But how? Is it because earthly desires make so much noise? And the dead have no desires; that only death purges us of our dishonesty, and that here, amongst the husbands, brothers, virgins and lovers are finally ranked no liars? - Every time we visit the war graves in France and Flanders fields I fall in love with the dead anew... I send up a silent prayer to them: 'Tell me what I have to do', I whisper – 'Show me how to live as fatally as you...')

Yes, I remember lots of things. Most of all: I remember my wife and I being happy. Kate's silence betrays her complicity in the mute deception of our post-natal discontent.

However modern we may be about the concept, relationships are a time-honoured arena in which romance and reality collide. Romance is a tall, flashy warrior whose victory is never in doubt – except in the end it's short and stubby reality that wins out. Romance, having worn himself out with the braggadocio of minor triumphs, passes out, leaving stocky reality to rob his corpse and throw the bugger out.

But of course, marriages change – all marriages: that's their distinguishing mark, their forte – indeed, their speciality. And it should say so on the box. 'Please be aware: this marriage will change: its contents will settle, and your happiness will weigh less.'

Actually, why is there no section of the 'trades descriptions act' that pertains to marriage? Why is this institution allowed to get away scot-free from the rigorous accuracy all other contractual engagements have to meet? If we knew marriage would change – and change us – would we still engage in the pursuit with such insane optimism? If we really knew marriages suffered grave alteration, maybe weddings, far from being events of unbridled joy and happiness would appropriately become far more funereal affairs, suffused with a profound sense of mourning at the impending loss of individuality and contentment about to be suffered by both parties? If we really knew....

Well, I can't deny something's changed in my marriage – and not for the better. But then it's been that way for years, on and off. And, as I say, how could it change for the better, when the best bit is self-consciously and triumphally the day when you get married? Everything else after that is a slow diminution of the spirit of celebration. Anniversaries merely inject marriage's flat champagne with cheap, gaseous verve again. But conscience isn't fooled. Conscience is the mind's digestive system: anniversaries cause flatulence and farting. That same flatulence and farting whose ugliness goes more and more unnoticed after marriage, but which, before the nuptials, would be guaranteed to prevent any engagement happening in the first place. Ask yourself: would you go out again with a man who farts repeatedly on the first date or two; the woman who burps unguardedly? I think not. But then marriage blunts the edge of our appetite for judgement and discretion.

The fact is that my bus driving test success confirms and magnifies the growing distance between Kate and me. I wish it didn't, but it does. She resents the fact that I resent the duty to bring home the Danish bacon in this way – which I do. Even though I have chosen it: I didn't have to leave the bank, leave Kate that first time when I.…

Contrary to what I said earlier, I have no perspective about this: I am reeling at having had to take this absurd job. Literally punch-drunk, I hear Kate encourage me at breakfast as if across a vast distance, from the galaxy of hope, but its twinkling circuitry of stars are light years away. I look at my small son, not from just across the room, but from across time itself. Slow melancholy waters rise against the floodgates of my eyes; I want to cry - but grief does not go with the uniform I'm about to wear. I say goodbye and exit for the depot under a mocking sun-drenched, cloudless sky.

∞

## 40 – The sound of breaking glass

The point I'm trying cack-handedly to make is that Auckland Avenue's broken window was for me a metaphor for consciousness the moment something else breaks into it – shatters it irrevocably. We all know these moments: bad news, the lover leaves, the doctor announces a deadly illness; someone you love 'breaks' into tears; you suffer heart-break, feel 'destroyed'.

Breakage is possibly *the* greatest metaphor for the human condition. We are so fragile; our constructions of our own happiness so prone to the elements. Everything about us begs to be shattered, bent out of shape, damaged, distorted, deformed, splintered, fractured and crushed. It's a wonder we bother to try and make anything of our lives when the basic materials at our disposal are so inherently flawed.

So are all breakages for the worse? Obviously not. Good things can also disrupt our barren rigidity; good fortune, health, love, money – yes, money – can break into your life with equal force. Like a breaking window in reverse, life can suddenly come back together – resolve into one perfect lens through whose magnifying glass you see only pellucid happiness! How wonderful, then, just to be alive, to breathe this colourless, odourless champagne ether called oxygen; to wander on cool carpets of grass, to dip fingers into languorous lakes, to... to....

The point is: fortune is a misnomer: chance and change are happening all the time. life is process – not stasis. If I may be allowed a Rimbaudian quip - life is a verb not a noun.

### 41 - First day out in the bus

*Insert keys. Turn ignition on. Exit the depot. Drive out into an ironic, unknown world of monstrous certainties! Here be dragons! I shall be affrighted!* There will be corners I can't cut, easy exits I can't negotiate! Customers I cannot placate!

Before I know it, I am driving through Croydon in a daze (is it possible do anything else in this godforsaken neck of the infernal suburban woods?) - And I am driving very slowly – too slowly: at the speed of a giant wheelbarrow.

'You'll have to pick it up a bit,' says the inspector – (they travel with you part of the way on your first day out) - 'or you won't get anywhere!'

I accelerate from ten to twenty miles an hour, which seems like Formula One speed in a bus in the High Street.

Then I stop to pick up my first ride. A bus stop full of 'spotty Herbert' schoolboys flashing bus passes at me with con-men's dexterity. Typically, the one I choose to pull back is valid for almost the full year ahead.

'Just got this done – can't you fuckin' read?' inquires said schoolboy.

His swearing is a knife jag'd deep into my sensibility. A weakness maybe, but I am not used to being sworn at by members of the public – at least not in this routinely vicious way that slashes first and asks questions later, leaving the victim (me) bleeding in a - doubtless - bourgeois pool of his own shock.

'Oy - you swear again and you're off the bus, my son: understand?' interjects my guardian angel inspector. The kid murmurs and presses his mates on down the aisle of the bus.

I feel safe with the inspector on board. But he's getting off in two more stops and then I'm on my own. The warfare on my equanimity that was promised now arrives: I hear the sound of violent teenage mockery - the slaughter has begun.

∞

## 42 – The mortal danger of empathy

But didn't I think I was going crazy? In Auckland Avenue, I mean. Surely I must've thought I was going crazy? Later, yes - with disastrous results. But not at the time. At that moment the whole thing, the 'event' (incidentally, a name I like less and less) just took me over, possessed me. I remember walking on down Auckland Avenue and realising 'someone is going to a singing lesson; now let's see what would that be like? How would it feel to be inside a musical note?' Music never disappoints.

Music! Our rescuer and refuge! Our sunlit escape route from the dark oubliette of personality! Music, that hauls us from the soul-sucking mire of our own emotional mediocrity! That slakes the parched throat with its sudden oasis. Music, at once so foreign and familiar, so full of exile and reunion! Music, so redolent of the lover's touch and stranger's stare. Music, at once so faithful and treacherous to both past and future.

Music, that abducts us blind and abandons us we know not where... Music...

As I walked through my singing teacher's door scales of piano notes rose and fell in the echo-chamber of my chest. Across the room stood my singing teacher. He said 'hallo' as if he were someone else. 'My' voice corrected him.

'You *are* me,' I replied.

He looked at me a little queerly to say the least (to use the strangely appropriate music-hall vernacular); but one can only tell these things as one sees them. And at that moment there was no difference between Stephen Marsh, respectable, absurdly bald, highly empathic singing teacher and me. Both of us were of one mind – whether he liked it or not.

'Oh my god, what's happened, Matthew? You've been on the sauce again, haven't you, you daft old tenor!'

Empathy is a dangerous thing: it can go too far: you can become the other person; identify with them so much you are absorbed by them, know their thoughts, feel their feelings – before they do.

'You know I've always felt enormous fondness for you, Stephen – even though you think I don't!' (Incidentally, though 'I' might have disappeared, I still used the language of 'I' and 'you'; I still knew that in order to use language there had to be division, a subject and object: you can't have a verb without a 'doer' and a 'done-to' of that verb.)

'And respect: I respect you enormously – even though you think I don't'.

'*Do* I think you don't?' inquired Stephen, somewhat taken aback by my knowledge of his deepest fears.

'I know we've disagreed at times - when the lessons don't go well.'

'Don't they go well?'

'Not all the time. You interrupt me too much.'

'Ah! - not 'interrupt – 'redirect'…

'Well… anyway, it doesn't matter. None of it does. Fact is, we're all mad!'

'Are we?'

'So why hide it? That's why I love coming here. Nothing's hidden. You *are* me. – And I am you - when we're in this room together.'

'And when we're not?' Stephen ventured tentatively.

'Who cares about that? This is all that matters. Singing in this room….'

'I see,' said Stephen, looking politely dazed.

And so, *because* I was Stephen, I too, instantly became confused – indeed, I suddenly plumbed the depths of Stephen's confusion, swam in their murky, translucent waters, seeing no further than a few feet in front of my own nose. Who knew what might rear up before us both as Stephen and I swam together in his confusion. Then there it was: a great big smile rearing up out of the depths: a smile as big as a dolphin's. Stephen was laughing. So I laughed. And there we were: laughing stupidly for its own sake. Ha! ha! ha! Hee! hee! hee! Ho! Ho! Ho! - Laughter is the wave of your own relief at life's absurdity breaking upon the shore of a rescued heart. How we laughed!

And then we didn't. Because Stephen fell silent. And so did I. profoundly, Pacifically, six-and-a-half mile deep Mariana trench-ly silent. At these depths our eyes shone like little monster beacons of light at each other. Human intimacy can survive at extraordinary depths where the pressure would kill any other species....

'Why don't we do some singing?' suggested the hitherto undiscovered deep-sea Stephen-fish.

'Why don't we!' I agreed. And so I sang - as never before or since.

### 43 – Mind like a cinema

*'Good luck! Take it slowly – but not too slow!' The inspector alights from my bus like a father abandoning his only son. Suddenly, I am alone.*

This is unreal. I want to get off the bus. Get out now! This joke has gone on long enough! I glance in my rear-view mirror at my passengers and see that nobody is laughing.

Then I do something stupid... I turn on my right indicator and engage 'drive'. An opening in the traffic comes and before I know it I am moving off! I am driving a bus in London! Am I mad? Then, scrabbling to turn off my indicators, I accidentally turn on the windscreen wipers on this starkly sunny day. Quickly extinguishing this betrayal of panic, I scrabble them off again and search the world in front of me. The glass offers no hiding-place.

Like a weird cinema, the bus's windscreen is a colossal, all-encompassing Imax of visual information – and it rattles sub-audibly: my impending panic is thus rendered in glorious Sensurround as well as Technicolor. I am suddenly the star of my own disaster movie – only there is no popcorn.

∞

## 44 – Here endeth the lesson...

How did the singing lesson end? I don't remember. How did the 'event' end? By fading. Imperceptibly like romance - like an acid trip ends – or perhaps with the re-emergence of time. Essentially, as I began to feel and see less, my senses starting drawing up a map of objects again, calculating distances between things, my hands from the tree's branches, my feet from my eyes... In this way, 'normal service' was resumed. All of a sudden, I found myself looking at my watch again. Funny little machine counting off the moments of eternity as if it owned them. Where does it go, this coinage of time so quickly lost from our possession? Apparently Buddhist monks aren't allowed to keep watches.... But then watches only really exist to tell us we're doing something boring; like hurrying, or being late or....

Put it this way: you only look at your watch if you've got to get somewhere, or if you're bored with where you are or what you're doing. You never, for instance, consult your watch during love-making. Indeed, if you're happy to be just where you are, to be doing just what you're doing; to stay, in effect, just where you are - for eternity - then time offers no useful reference; ceases, in fact, to be of any use; time ceases, in fact, to be.

Similarly, it strikes me that eternity is not some hackneyed state of un-endingness stretching out before us, but rather an internal state of mind *outside time* altogether. What we call the 'eternal' is really no more than this experience of time-less-ness.

We all have this, we all experience parts of our lives when time is suddenly irrelevant, transcended; as, for example, occurs in the company of close friends and lovers, or a beloved piece of music. Later we look up and see half an hour has just vanished; or two hours; or maybe, if we're abroad in a special sunlit town or landscape we love, two weeks will disappear, or a whole summer - without reference to a clock or watch. Thus we slip in and out of time all the time, without really appreciating our miraculous talent for so doing; for being shape-shifters who can easily manipulate this, perhaps the most basic element of our lives – time.

Perhaps the implications are too much to bear, because if we can do all this pretty much unconsciously; what might we not do were we to train our powers, like, say, the magi of old who sat deep in meditation in their caves?

But of course, caves have gone out of fashion, and so have magi. Even the memory of them seems more than faintly ludicrous; indeed, we have been persuaded of their absurdity by the scientific spirit of time; time that tells us only the hands of the clock can be relied upon to point out our direction in life. Personally, I suspect it is clock-time that lies....

So as I walked back home along Auckland Avenue, gradually the evening shadows lengthened; distance grew back between me and the trees; flowers lost their radiance, became colourful rather than luminous, became merely pleasant again, rather than part of an electrified ambience; and the sun, the setting sun began to float down and away - like a red balloon drifting tragically out of my reach.

## 45 – Life blurred

*Streets pass in a blur. I stop at empty bus-stops, speed past full ones!*

'Oy driver, are you thinking of stopping any time today – we wanna get off!' a joker wise-cracks from the central aisle. I raise my hand in a pseudo-calm gesture of apology and stop the bus to allow their descent. Then, without further explanation to the passengers, I yank off the handbrake, grate the auto into 'drive' and set off with a lurch that unsettles a row of shopping bags on the shelf next to the disabled seats; their contents of bread, sugar, tea, milk and cornflakes serving up an untimely breakfast to the elderly who occupy them. Generously, I do not charge extra for this.

∞

## 46 – What time is it? What, is it time? What is it: time..?

'What do you mean "you disappeared"?' Kate inquired with a mysterious blend of dispassionate irritability. She was tired out. Her pregnancy had been fraught with prolonged sickness and predictably my attempt to explain Auckland Avenue was now crashing and burning in front of its first audience.

'What I mean is the 'I' we normally think we experience – just wasn't there anymore – at least not for while.'

'So what *was* there?'

'Everything. Insanely powerfully....'

'"Everything"' Right.... And where were you then. No, don't tell me – "everywhere".

'Yes, in a manner of speaking. – And *nowhere*. It was like I died... but it didn't matter. It was... the most peaceful I've ever felt ---'

'Peaceful... to be dead!' Kate is unimpressed with this interpretation of mortality.

'Yes. Time doesn't exist.'

'Oh no? Well I think you'll find it's just gone six forty-five.'

'Death doesn't exist.'

'Matt --- '

'What I mean is – death only exists if time exists. If time – our *experience* of time ceases to exist, then we cease to exist. Time only measures finite things. Don't you see?'

'No, I don't.'

'Look, you're not listening, Kate – please. If I can't make you understand ---'

'Make me?'

'I'm just saying... the bank  - work – I think I need a change....'

'Matt, I'm five months pregnant!'

'All I'm saying is this changes things. Don't you see?' At this point I took Kate gently by the shoulders. Surely this experience was pretty straightforward? It seemed straightforward to me.... That's how mad it was.

'Matt, let me go.'

'Kate ---'

'For chrissake get off!'

Belatedly, idiotically, I realised how upset she was, and how absurd I was to expect her to make any sense of my feeble narrative. We fell silent and surrendered to mutual incomprehension.

Kate went to bed early that evening. On my own downstairs in the flat I sat in the dark – both actually and metaphorically. The silence seemed peculiarly, eerily intense. I wondered if this was what deafness, blindness was like. Then it struck me – and with it a kind of fear – that I was on my own with this one.

### 47 – Don't sweat it

*I am sweating. I am sweating like never before - like no human being has ever sweated before.* I am the perspiration equivalent of Louis the fourteenth. I am the sweat king of Europe! And my passengers are my hapless subjects Appropriately, revolution seems to be fomenting behind me. Suddenly an old woman dressed in a regulation turquoise mac disturbs the silent ecstasy of my panic, berating me:

'Driver, you've gone the wrong way!' What? In life? I want to reply.

'No! Look! Go down Urquhart Street – down here; that's where we go! Are you asleep?' No, madam (my "thought-bubbles" burble back), I am comatose with fear, which is much worse.

'I do apologise, madam, I'm just getting used to the new route.'

'Yes, well it's not new to us, so if you'd kindly let us off…!'

I prepare to do so, but brake too hard, this time causing a small landslide of briefcases, umbrellas and bags down the bus's central aisle. But this is no time to study the geology of indignation unearthed upon the faces of my passengers....

∞

## 48 – Mother, Ronnie and other sceptics

And then, of course, there was mother...

After Auckland Avenue I rang her in a fit of naivety, thinking she might be interested in the strangest – and yet simultaneously most harmonious - experience in the hitherto profoundly discordant music of her son's life....

Mistake. She laughed. Said she didn't know what I was on, but could I get her some of it? No, mother couldn't't've cared less about what happened in Auckland Avenue: she was too busy having her own hallucinations. Up or down – everything was a trip for mother. Like most addicts, her mind was a chemistry set in the hands of a child; her moods were playthings. Colours, sounds and sensations constituted her only source of value. Addicts are not into the significance of their experiences, caring only that they should blow themselves clean away; they're not interested in how or why they absent themselves from infelicity awhile, so long as they can hang the sign up 'out to lunch each and every day'.

'What did you expect? Your mother's a junkie.' Kate confirmed unequivocally.

Back at the bank I also tried to tell Ronnie about Auckland Avenue.

'You what?'

'Look: whatever you may think, Ronnie, the fact is I've had... an experience...'

'Yeah, well we've all had one of those mate! – 'Listen, I took Suzanne out to ---'

'No, an experience without a woman in it, Ronnie... - a serious experience...'

This was, of course, a contradiction in terms for Ronnie. There was - *could be* - no serious experience without a woman in it, or, should I say, no worthwhile experience without Ronnie in a woman.

No, Ronnie turned away glassy-eyed after a few minutes as I clumsily set out my stall of the otherworldly event. In fact, that market-day marked the day when Ronnie turned away for good. Ronnie was not a buyer at such stalls. He was only too happy with earthly experience – and why not, when it sold him all he needed – or thought he needed.

But I'm venturing on the priggish – which is always a danger with this kind of experience; as if it somehow sets you not only apart from other people – which it does – but above them too – which it very definitely doesn't.

In reality, what can I say about Auckland Avenue that makes any sense?

Maybe I *am* crazy. That said, I'm not, by nature, given to fantasies of whatsoever kind. I don't believe in peace and love on earth (I'd like to, but 800,000 years of upright human history weigh heavily against the feasibility of the ideal); I have no history of so-called mental problems; I don't hear voices (would that I did, it'd all be so much easier to explain); I have never suffered from depression or hysteria; I do not labour under the delusion of my own religious sanctity or grandeur. I am certainly no saint, and, like most of my absurdly guilt-ridden North-European protestant brothers and sisters, I am only a modest sinner.

### 49 – Boiled-sweet-coloured traffic lights

*Great god in beacon-heaven. Traffic lights! Is there no end to them!? Stop. Go. Stop. Stop, Go. Stop….. Gooooooo… - Gaudy baubled necklaces of prohibition and permission!* The adult's childish guide to success or failure on life's great highway. Green, green, green, stay green my lovelies – stay green! Green, green, green, stay green – stay green – Bitch! Orange! At the last moment! Those last few yards when it's obvious you've got time to stop; when it'd be absurd to pretend you hadn't seen them or didn't have time to stop. Orange lights: you can't break them, but on their own minor level their indigestible boiled sweets leave you choking for air! Red. Red lights. Stop. Stop. Stop!

Fluency is a lovely word. It sounds... fluent. It flows from one's mouth out into the air. It bespeaks onward motion, the promise of the future. I have none. Only traffic lights that imprison me in an eternal statically interrupted present tense – a time without time that gradually stretches across the whole morning – until, at last I reach my turnaround point. I can stop.

My last passengers get off. I turn off the engine. Its wicked laughter dies in its throat. I have thirty minutes to recover before setting off again.

∞

## 50 – A pendulum of questions

In the days after Auckland Avenue, all I got was questions.

How was it possible that such an event happened to me at all? How could a definitively normal life such as mine give rise to an abnormal, extraordinary experience? Surely everything must have a cause, must be produced by a cause? What, then, was the cause of the event in Auckland Avenue? Did it lie back in my past - in the furthest reaches of childhood – and beyond..?

And here, try as I might to resist its use, the dread word 'karma' rears its ugly 'hippy-dippy' head. I mean, we've all heard the word, we all to some extent grasp the principle of so-called 'Dependent Origination', as Oriental scholars paraphrase 'Karma': the idea that one's own personal behaviour is like a chain in which a series of acts link one to another. But I certainly don't recall anything in childhood that would've led to Auckland Avenue; no chain of psychological links connecting my past to the extraordinary event that hit me in that profoundly ordinary street. But maybe karma has nothing to do with it? Maybe it's something much more simple? Maybe, in the case of Auckland Avenue, it's more a question of the pendulum effect: the idea that over the years your behaviour veers so much in one direction that after a while it can't help swinging back in the other?

What if the soul, as well as matter, obeys Newton's law; what if, energetically-speaking, every immoral action produces an equal and opposite reaction in the heart? In that sense, couldn't despair point up the way back to joy, and wrongdoing lead to contrition? Didn't the great sinners have their moments of redemption just after sinning? I'm not saying it always happens, because, of course, that'd mean murderers effortlessly turned into angels... just that it might in some individuals.... Where, when you think about it, does conscience come from?

### 51 - Un-beauty spot

*Time glides by cinematically like the endless series of shop windows my bus passes.* And so afternoon itself passes – or so I am led to believe - because I am conscious of none of it. My mind is locked in a rictus of dumb panic, a frozen hysteria from which my rigid arms reach out to receive money, turn knobs on and off, and turn a steering wheel this way and that. Suddenly I see the depot ahead. It is over! Except it isn't.

Right at the end of my route, just before turning into the depot, I mildly collide with a head-high road-sign. Actually, the damage is minimal, though the clash and gash of metal bus and sign shocks my older passengers, as though a bomb has just gone off. I have to stop the bus to take details - and apologise... sort of.

'Wicked! You've mashed the fuckin' bus mate!" as one kind-hearted punter has the good grace to inform me on stepping off the platform.

I will also have to report this myself. You have to log all incidents – major and minor. The company operate a sort of 'three strikes and you're out' policy whereby they can sack the more accident-prone.

But this mishap is behind me, and so at last is my first day. Back in the shade of the depot. I almost fall out of my bus with relief. Across the yard, Phil the Janitor looks up and unfortunately bears witness to my ineptitude. Bollocks to him. Bollocks to everyone and everything. Bollocks, above all, to me.

∞

## 52 – Karma

I'm really only trying to figure out what could have produced the event in Auckland Avenue in me, other than some inexplicable influence exerted by my own past.... Certainly, I saw nothing in my character that predicted any such experience. And this being the case, how could something one can't recall exert or enact any influence upon the present? By what agency? And why? It seems inexplicable. And yet our own childhoods, so little of which we really remember, certainly haunt us in the guise of our current temperaments and attitudes. Didn't that brilliant old bore Wordsworth declare 'the child is father of the man'?

Maybe that's precisely what they mean by this mysterious law of Karma: actions, moods, feelings, thoughts in previous lives come back to haunt you. I can see how that might operate in the same life – but over different ones? That's stretching it. How could karma work to connect the pattern of lives? Doesn't everything stop at death? Isn't the world flat, after all? Don't we sail over the ocean of life to plunge into death's abyss? Or maybe something mysterious happens in death to join us to the next life, maybe urgently odd things happen down at the deathly bottom of our own spiritual version of the Mariana Trench, seven miles deep in our psyches? The depths and the darknesses we inhabit certainly harbour strange forces and beasts. Sharks are five hundred million years old. And we're all related to the things of the sea – who knows what lies down inside us – in the depths of our death? Conversely, of course, karma, like human nature, is not all sinister forebodings! Good actions, thoughts and feelings produce happy results. Karma could be a school of dolphins carrying you home!

## 53 – Ronnie's Anglo-Saxon hermeneutics

I don't ask these questions for show, but rather to try and understand how a life as profoundly ordinary as mine can suddenly undergo such a revolutionary turning about in the deepest seat of consciousness. Exactly what is it that produces a change of heart in a life without meaning? Then again, what's wrong with a life without meaning? Nothing – according to Ronnie... to whom I nonsensically insisted on trying to explain the event in Auckland Avenue.

'Look, can I just stop you there a minute, mate?' Ronnie asked rhetorically as he interrupted me. 'Firstly, I haven't got a fucking clue what you're on about. Secondly, I'm not sure you have either...'

'I'm talking about...what's there when you – or the 'you' you think you are – suddenly disappears...' I protested.

'I'll tell you what's there – fuck-all!' Ronnie asseverated (and Ronnie never asseverated unless he meant it).

I had to agree. Actually, looking back, Ronnie's honest Anglo-Saxon analysis, comically fusing a positive and negative as it did, provided a consummately ironic encapsulation of what had happened in Auckland Avenue.

## 54 - The writing on the depot wall

*So, finally back at the depot, Day One is done – and already the writing's on my wall. With any luck I may not make it through the first month at all!* Another nail in my coffin is the fact that I have also taken too little cash for a normal day on this particular route; let too many fare-dodgers through my grasp. But the company expect that in Week One. Do it again in Week Two and Three and, of course, you're out. We can but hope.

Above all, I may not make it through because a sharp spike of mental fatigue has drilled its way into the core of my consciousness every hour, draining me of every last reserve of energy – now, by evening, it has hit the bedrock of my being - and struck nothing. For nothing is what is left of me after the first day driving, pinned – like a crucified Vitruvian man – to the wheel of this behemoth as it sits monstrously silent, beached on the dark shore of the depot. I stagger out. Jonah is disgorged at last.

∞

## 55 – Mind out of time

Time is – so we are told – above all, money… especially when working for an investment bank. So, in the wake of Auckland Avenue, I thought I'd take some myself… time, I mean: commandeer some unpaid leave. I demanded three weeks off! (I don't know why three exactly, perhaps just because it seemed more significant than a fortnight, which is just for flashy vacations in Phuket). Anyway, I told the bank I'd leave if they didn't let me. Kate was both relieved and concerned. So was I. All of a sudden I no longer knew if I was coming or going, principally because I was doing both.

I thought time off would restore me. A bit of time to myself.

Nature. I would spend some time with this old goddess, see what she had to say to me, or I to her. I went to the Lake District for the weekend. This was entirely selfish of course, since, though a few weeks away yet, Kate's pregnancy was moving inexorably towards its due date. Still, Kate exonerated me by insisting she'd go and stay with her mum.

'You go.' she said, scarcely able to conceal her relief at getting rid of her crazy, mixed-up, suddenly useless man. ' Sort your head out.'

'Only if you're sure...'

'We'll be fine.... Go. Find one of those bloody forests you love!'

So I did.

## 56 - Into the forest

Forests are cool. I mean literally. Metaphorically, too, of course. Forests occupy a special place in the hearts of men and women. In forests everything cools down, slows down; in forests you come upon the time to be yourself - whatever or whoever that is, or proves to be.

Ironically, I didn't walk alone in the forests of the Lake District because mother followed me - in spirit. She had a habit of turning up when least expected – or desired.

When I was a kid, during those Halcyon hours when the syringe had just done its work mother could occasionally be very loving. She might tell me to come close and stroke my hair, or whisper blurred maternal affections, call me her knight-in-armour (one birthday I'd been bought a silver, plastic suit of the stuff and proudly wore it – for just a few months too long, when some kid laughed at it and I never put it on again. It's a chilling moment in life when you realise others have just seen right though your disguise.)

Of course, coming down from a high was quite another matter. Sometimes, when things got especially bad with mother, I'd retreat into a nearby wood with the little terrier I'd been given by one of her blokes. Actually, in doing this I was following the one piece of decent advice mother ever gave me:

'Take that fucking dog and get out of my sight!' she would sagely counsel.

So I did. No doubt the dog reminded her of Johnnie, her useless bloke at the time. Johnnie was a 'traveller' not that he ever seemed to travel very far, Balham marking the outer limit of his bucolic vagabondage, as I recall. But Johnnie I liked. He always had a pack of dogs in train, and had given me this one, unpeeling its lead from the fistful he held in his hand. Like a little canine balloon, the dog floated off in my childish hand. Such is the sky-ward fate of man's best friend. Scarcely less at the behest of the god of circumstance myself, I would drift with my beloved dog into the nearby wood.

In the forest I would think about mother; how much I hated her, how much I wanted not to be with her. And then slowly, intangibly and invisibly, by dint of the forest's mysterious powers of distraction and abstraction, my hurt would disappear.

Play heals. Not just actual childish play, the floating of paper boats, the building of dams and bridges made out of stones and twigs, which, like any child, I loved – but, as my teens wore on into adulthood, their mature imaginary equivalents: the mind's play – and the heart's ease therein.

In the forest the unthreatened play of thoughts and feelings brings the spirits out. Everything comes closer. Like fallow deer, one's deepest instincts and intuitions scent one out, sniff the air for a true sight and sound of who one is. So, too, one's most intimate sentiments, for so long affrighted by the noise one makes in the outer world, so long menaced by the sight of one's own face, approach and enter into a ring of subtle confidence.

In the forest one thus becomes a kind of hermit at the centre of one's own mystic world, a universe in which nothing is excluded, and all things are related to each other by a common bond of empathy: the tacitly accepted reflection in each other's eyes. In the forest no-one is afraid to look each other in the eyes. Is this the poet's world? That sense of power and peacefulness comingled?

Of course, such a forest need not be geographical; it may be anywhere you feel at peace; may be in the high street or the City square; may be in the eyes of the beloved you accidentally meet. In this sense the poet's words, his fallow deer, may wander unnoticed and unharmed, protected by the aura of their own peacefulness in the raucous, midnight urban street.

Of course, I couldn't stay in the actual forest all day - certainly not all cold night long. I had to go home, where I would usually find mother lying in a stupor on the sofa, with the TV switched on holding a conversation with itself. If it was daytime it would be discussing antiques, or staging a melodramatic dialogue between some girlfriend and boyfriend, before rushing out in tears to the tune of soap opera credits. Or at night the television might be brooding silently, as trivially intense men sat gleaming round a spot-lit table playing poker in the televised darkness. I loved that green baize table: it stood like a small green clearing of hopefulness amid the cluttered chaos of mother's life – a miniature echo of the purity of the forest I'd just left. To this day, if I'm driving, to see shafts of sunlight stripe the dark forest trees with swathes of gold causes me a kind of beautiful pain; sometimes I have to stop the car and walk awhile just to clear my mind of memories of mother - and be at ease again...

## 57 – The burn-out suns of the South of France

*During that first week driving the bus the streets are a metallic forest I enter every day.* More than the route I track, my own desperate concentration is a vertiginous path I keep to. Each hour is an abyss I may plunge into; time, itself, a cliff-face: I cling to the weeds of its minutes. How? With the intensity that a fear of humiliation exerts; that and my 'bottom line' desperate need for cash - I certainly hang on to that.

So the first weeks shade into the first month. My profane baptism of bus-lane fire suddenly done, my first paycheque arrives and lo and behold: I am not earning £500 a week with overtime! Because I am, of course, too exhausted to do any overtime. And the time I am doing is slow, like prison-time.

On getting home after my shift I begin to get into the habit of going straight to bed – forgetting to kiss my son goodnight. Predictably, on this account, one morning Kate shoots me an ugly look.

'So this is how it's gonna be, is it?' I look up from my dismal piece of toast. 'You going all silent on us, ignoring your baby son? Staring at the wall all day long!'

'Look don't start. I haven't got time.'

'Well, make time, Matt! Make time to kiss your son goodnight. It only takes a fucking moment!'

'I did kiss him.' Lies buy time in arguments.

'No you fucking didn't!' Exhausted mothers are like dying stars: they burn out in an implosive, atomic blaze of 'f' words. 'You didn't even go into his fucking room!'

'Well I meant to.'

'Meant to? What fucking good is that? I "meant" to marry a millionaire, I "meant" to live in the fucking South of France!'

I stare into my tea cup. She's right. "The fucking South of France..." That part of France where all the fucking goes on – where *only* fucking goes on. No we were not living in the fucking South of France of the mind. We were living in fucking Lewisham, where we ourselves were royally fucked – and not in a good way.

'Look, I've got to go.... I'm sorry. I won't forget tonight.' I slide out of the room and the house like a shadow cast by a closing door.

Thus ends the first of an increasing number of such encounters that begin to mark the trench warfare of the marital home at morning, noon and night.

And there is something else: I don't feel right. My stomach is uncomfortable; I have to urinate two or three times a night – and my bowel movements are shifting weirdly: once as regular as a tedious mantelpiece clock, they now insist on sudden evacuations with very little warning. But of course, if I ignore this it will simply go away.

∞

## 58 – To hell with nature

The Lakes and their forests were beautiful of course. This made returning from them even worse. The following week my sense of disharmony became unbearably intense: the dissonance between what Auckland Avenue represented and my life in The City. My trouble was that I wanted – desperately needed - to transpose one on top of the other, to carry 'the event' with me into my daily, quotidian, banal life at the bank. But 'normal' life wasn't having it. Normal life was happy as it was. Wasn't it? But hadn't the event actually happened in Auckland Avenue: bastion of banality?! Backdrop to the most mysterious event of my life! As such, normal Auckland Avenue had broken every rule, contradicted every cliché – especially what 'normally' happens in such experiences, at least the ones we read about

Looking back, in Auckland Avenue I had not been not 'at one with nature' – at least not in the corny sense. People, old hippies, mainly, ramble on about 'connectedness' and 'being one with nature'; this is fine as far as it goes, but implies a subtle, misanthropic solipsism, not to mention a certain phenomenalistic chauvinism. After all, why just nature? What about 'being one' or 'at one' with the city, its people, and boring objects such as iron railings, bollards and asphalt? Wouldn't a truer version of connectedness include all these?

Of course, I only thought such thoughts in retrospect. At the time, in Auckland Avenue, I thought no thoughts at all. I was too busy pushing the sun gently about the sky.

And I know I've said enough about flowers – but *can you* say enough about flowers? The vanity of flowers is both ridiculous and beautiful. Fortunately, their penchant for display exceeds normal adapted behaviour. The flower's whole existence is pathologically engineered and geared for self-love – and we love them for it. How else, without such attention to the detail of their own loveliness, would flowers become so beautiful? Even corporation flower beds, wherein councils try so hard to neuter the passionate, incontinent vanity of the flower, cannot wholly mask the truth of the fertility of this blasphemous self-love.

I speak from personal experience as a flower. Yellow is a feeling of ecstasy; Purple, of intense elegance, and Green is tranquillity – but Red? Red is the colour of dynamic contemplation or deeply creative sleep. No coincidence that the poppy is red; that its opium sends us into deeply vivid dreams. In Auckland Avenue, none of these colours could I hold at arm's length: to see them was immediately to be them.

Maybe that's as it should be. Life held at arm's length is no life at all; similarly, the flower merely classified botanically defies any real, lasting or deep communion. Conversely, when you really look with intimacy, gaze intensely like a lover, you cease to be conscious of the line of demarcation between you and the flower; realise your shared power, process and beauty. Maybe that's part of what that man called Buddha meant when he silently held up the flower in front of his disciples and awaited their dumbfounded response in vain. 'Thou art that', he said - at least according to old-fashioned academics' somewhat biblical translations. Conversely, when one of the Buddha's followers suddenly smiled a brilliant smile at the held-up flower, the man called Buddha un-biblically burst out 'Kondanna's got it! Yes, he's got it!' (Similar to Rex Harrison and Audrey Hepburn in My Fair Lady, but with culturally more significant implications – certainly if you value the sudden invention of Zen).

All this might sound somewhat delusional, I grant you: but doesn't the same unification happen to the painter? Doesn't Turner become the stormy seas? Don't their powers redound to his brush, flow in his veins? Isn't Michelangelo at the hypersensitive fingertip spark of creativity itself as Adam reaches out to God on the Sistine Chapel ceiling?

How else should we relate to nature, to the so called 'objective' world of experience, if not by transcribing the music of its powers, by harmonising our humanity with its meaning? Our seed, too, is sown, we ripen, flourish and die away. A gentian is nothing unless you feel the beauty of its blueness; the lilac dull unless its fragrance intoxicates; nature itself is lifeless unless you bend with the heavy burden of the bee that bows your fragile petal.

In this deepest sense, Imagination (with a capital 'I') is empathy; namely, that you become and understand what you imagine, and are thus intimately related to everything that happens to you. Indeed, in an inverted and very real sense, it is *you* who are happening to *it*. You *are* existence. In that sense, everything is imagination. There *is* nothing else. Ask William Blake, English pioneer and champion of man's defining faculty....

## 59 – Blood

*I've been driving over this bridge for a month now: from the cabin of my bus I gain a brief panorama of London and the river :– old Father Thames! Did your city flourish over the millennia in exactly the form that you foresaw?* Did we, your sons and daughters? As a bus-driver I am the keeper of a lock: I regulate a flow of humanity: passengers enter the bus like a sluice-gate opened. Their slow relentless flood swells the central aisle – but there's something more to this one on the bridge, something more turbulent about their current.

A group of boys are already jostling as they get on board. As a veteran of nearly seven weeks' driving experience, I feel like an old lag where youthful bad behaviour is concerned. But violence – real violence – has a distinctive quality. It rears its monstrous head with demon speed and suddenly time moves at a different pace – simultaneously imperceptibly fast – yet also in slow motion.

'Lads, can you quieten down a bit. The passengers can't hear themselves speak...' I announce over the PA system.

Further jostling; now some serious swearing – more than a row.

'Lads, I'm not moving the bus until --- '

The raised voice of real alarm has a distinct timbre to it; pain, real pain, has its own ironically clipped, staccato music. I look sharply in my mirror to see one of the boys has dropped to the floor. His assailants suddenly bolt for the door. Think quick! I could close it – lock them in! What? So they can stab the rest of us? For chrissake, let them go! Let them escape this minor chaos, let them out into the greater chaos, the chaotic anonymity of the street. Rightly or wrongly I open the doors – several youths disperse, one laughing.

A girl's scream, visceral panic rends the air.

The boy is bleeding – not uncontrollably, but steadily, in a way that demands a serious response.

I hear - I really hear – myself asking 'is there a doctor on the bus?'

Amazingly, there is. A young woman, surely not long out of grad' school, comes down from a seat on the top floor of the bus and asks people to step aside to give the boy air. For the split second I can afford my own sense of decency I find her very attractive: she is dark-haired, pretty and saves people's lives – what more can one ask of one's fare-paying customers?

Her cool-eyed assessment is that though the small puncture-wound to his thigh does not appear life-threatening he needs immediate ambulance attention. I stumble back to my cabin and issued a code red.

A 'code red' is an emergency call through to the main London control centre. They then contact the nearest hospital and get assistance. As the bus-driver you have to wait, whilst asking the remaining passengers to get off and catch the next bus.

Understandably, charity only extends so far. Knowing the boy isn't going to die, a different orchestra strikes up. Pain's dark music starts to be modulated by the thin violin strains of trivial moans about lateness and inconvenience, suggestions that the youths shouldn't have been let on the bus in the first place.

Panic over. The ambulance comes. The paramedics are like uniformed angels who descend to earth, resolve our pain, wrap it up and take it away. So they do with this soldier of the streets, taking away this mock 'gangsta in the 'hood', this urban rebel against boredom, away - leaving me to clear up his blood as I await the police.

You can lose an awful lot of blood in a very short time, as this boy has - apparently without much of a problem – except for the one who has to clear it up.

A pint, was it? I stood and looked at it. This blood. This thick red sauce, this human pomodoro inexplicably poured over no pasta. What was I supposed to do with it? I had only a small cloth and in a couple of seconds it had absorbed all that cloths are interested in. Cloths are part-timers really, not serious about the job they've been engaged to do; cloths are clock-watchers with no sense of vocation; they do the bare minimum and then disappear. In a sense I can see where they're coming from. I've been a cloth myself, I know what a lousy job it can be to clear up other people's shit. And then what's in it for them..?

So, now cloth-less, I stared at the blood – and the blood stared back, daring me to do nothing.

Blood in any quantity is warm to the touch - too warm - as if alive. I don't want to touch it, precisely because it has an uncanny life of its own, as if, at any moment, it might rear up; as if it wanted to get back into the body that had accidentally spilled it; wanted to get home...

117

Blood outside the body is an orphan, it cries for its parent. I could put my arm around it but I could not reunite them, these closest of relations, body and blood.

Of course, the police arrived and bollocked me politely for interfering with a crime scene. Anyway, there was nothing further I could do and the bus was now in the hands of forensics.

I stepped down from my cabin and gazed at the river – and old Father Thames gazed back impassively, with no tears in his eyes, having seen it all before.

I turned away and waited for another bus myself....

∞

## 60 – The word 'why' as an irrepressible Corsican peasant

'For chrissake, can't you stop moping?'

With her accusative question, Kate made me realise that I was doing it again in public – 'moping', I mean. I have always been a good moper: proud of my ability, even on the busiest of days, to find time for a quick practise of this old Scandinavian dialect word 'mopa' – 'to sulk'. Yes, I was moping. And I was not to be deterred from my modern expertise in this timeless vice, this priceless Nordic gift to the world.

'I'm not moping,' I replied, mopily.

Kate saw, of course, that The Lakes had solved nothing. I had grown morose, my conversation clipped, even abrupt at times. In response, Kate began to go out quite a lot - saw old friends; left me to contemplate my position - but I was sick of the practise; sick of the tools of the trade, sick of its principal piece of equipment – *the word 'why'* - Why had it happened? Why me? Me: so respectably normal in my ambitions; so reasonably greedy, so predictably, modestly bourgeois in my desire for women, wine and song.

'Why?'

Such a shitty little word – it ought to be ignored. Unfortunately it has Napoleonic pretensions. Indeed, who can deny that, having come from such humble beginnings, such a modest background in the lowest ranks of verbal intercourse and culture, the word 'why' has, over the centuries, risen in importance to take over the whole world of human meaning. Yes, this little Napoleon 'why', this Corsican peasant amongst words, has, when all is said and done, set its own precedent: 'why' is what gives the world meaning. If we couldn't ask 'why' there wouldn't be any need for meaning, any capacity to feel a need for it. Things would just happen without reason. The good would die young and evil would triumph – or appear to – and no-one would care... because that would be just the way it was.

Unfortunately – or fortunately, depending upon your optimism or cynicism - this little general amongst words thrust itself forward into consciousness, showed its cunning and bravery at vital moments, got promoted from the ranks to commander-in-chief of self-importance - and here we all are: living under its military yoke, serving its commands to invade the continent of insignificance and spread the plague of meaning everywhere. 'Why' has thus planted its French flag, its tricolour of meaning far and wide, until we all speak its blood-stained language. I certainly do. Indeed, I stand in its lowly ranks of questioners.

Why, indeed, *did* the event in Auckland Avenue happen to me? Then again, why do I even need to ask why? - Why 'why'? What is the meaning of meaning, et cetera, et cetera...

I can only answer that we are congenitally cursed with the primal need to transpose meaning onto our world, and thus, concomitantly, born with the capacity to ask why. Conversely, a world without meaning would be an act of heartless, superficial cruelty – or 'Hollywood', as it is sometimes called.

No - I am human, therefore I need meaning; therefore I ask 'why'. 'Je suis humain, donc, j'ai besoin de sens; donc, je me demand pourquoi...' as Descartes meant to say.

Pulling on my clinician's prosaic, white coat for a moment, I might put it aetiologically, and say that experience causes an internal wound because of our spiritual leukaemia, and that to be human is to be bruised repeatedly and lose a lot of blood. The question 'why' is, in this context, a blood transfusion machine; the blood being meaning. The word 'why' thus works to transfuse us with the vital, healthy blood of meaning until such time as we can cleanse ourselves of the deficiency, the leukemic cancer of meaninglessness that flows in our veins...

Nothing else requires this kind of transfusion. No other creature suffers from this life-threatening deficiency of meaning. Do wombats require meaning? Sharks? Dogs? Does the dog have Buddha-nature? – as medieval Eastern monks used to wonder in the centuries before technology rendered these sort of questions absurd.

Anyway, maybe meaning for a wombat is the gratification of its daily needs as it tunnels from burrow to burrow, eating its favourite plants. Maybe the human wombat is no better – until it stops and asks itself 'why do I live down here in the dark? What would happen if I went up top and lived up there forever? Would the leaves be juicier, the female wombats easier to pursue? Shall I stay or shall I go? What do you, my fellow wombat, think that I should do?

After the event in Auckland Avenue, the predicament of wombats took on new meaning for me.

### 61 - The joys of nostalgia

*The night following the stabbing I wake up in a sweat – nightmares have been fairly frequent visitors in the first couple of months driving; but the nightmares are never about the bus: that would be too simple.* In this incubus, my mother is hitting me in a rage. The look on her face exudes a quality of malice that terrifies my dormant adult sensibility so that I have never been more glad to wake and see the dawn (as they say in 19th century Gothic novels. Actually, life is a Gothic novel, our modern myopia means we simply fail to recognise its Northanger Abbey proportions).

Next morning, then, at breakfast, I turn over a few thoughts with the letters from that day's post, and the news in one of them floods the Thames Barrier of my waking consciousness with last night's dream again. My sister, my always shadowy relationship with whom had, in recent years, fallen into the dusky half-light of infrequent contact, had written to tell me that mother had died. Simple – and infinitely complex – as that.

∞

## 62 – Your own personal BC & AD

No doubt about it: Auckland Avenue was my Year Zero experience. We may not write it down, but each one of us contains within us his or her own water-shed dates. We are the timelines of our own myth and mystery on which are marked our inner crises, our 'BC's and 'AD's – our dates before and after our own greatly intimate events; our hearts before we fell in and out of love; our souls before we cast out our demon, or embraced him;

slew the dragon or were slain; our consciences before we woke and realised we'd been asleep for centuries.

Imagine the *opposite* of alcohol, the *opposite* of a hangover: you've drunk too much clarity to see things through the necessary fog that so-called 'normal' life demands; try as you might to accept your normal state of mental slumber, you just can't shake off the barely suppressed memory of quiet elation that pervades your body, speech and mind. You realise that, far from being circumscribed by your own restrictive limitations, there is an infinitely larger world which lies intimately near to you, one which delivers extraordinary sensations and feelings into your grasp; in fact, in reality you *are* only those sensations. It's like that moment when the jet you're in climbs above the curtain of British clouds and you see that all the while the world has been saturated with blue sky and sun – your point-of-view was just set too low down to see it.

### 63 - Funeral Emotions

*Only a couple of months into driving the bus and I have to ask for compassionate leave off to attend mother's funeral. This they give me grudgingly, perhaps doubting I actually have – or ever had – a mother.*

I will go to mother's funeral alone. Kate decides not to come. Mother and she had never got on. No, that's a lie respectably disguised in a cliché – they had loathed each other. Added to which emotional antipathy was the practical consideration of our son: six month old babies and funerals don't mix.

So I journey to Bristol on my own. The sky is heavily overcast with charcoal shaded clouds: one of those wintery days whose dungeon light flares briefly only to foreshadow the return of dusk. It made me shiver.

Why this fear of the dark? Of the dead? How can they hurt us? Why this respect for them, when we never held them dear in life? *If* we never held them dear in life... and it had been years since I had held my own mother dear. And now, suddenly, this letter in my hands, telling me of my mother's death; and suddenly it is too late to cross this deep lacuna between my past and present, too late to redress this lack, address this wound.

Was it a wound? What did I really feel for this woman? Did I feel anything anymore for a mother who had, doubtless, with many mitigating factors, perpetrated the act of motherhood upon me with such casual disregard for my own – or her - safety? My childhood had, as I say, been a repeated accident always about to happen.

'The train now careering to a stop at platform four calls at disappointment, frustration and despair; join the last four carriages for physical as well as mental pain...'

But that branch line was long behind me now. Or so I'd thought. Until now, when apparently it holds one more journey in store for me....

No matter how modern the rolling stock, train journeys are so irremediably old-fashioned! There's something about this antiquated mode of transport – the primitive, rhythmic clackety-clack the track percussion makes, the engine literally hauling coupled carriages along in its wake! No, trains remain inviolably locked in the 19th century: one's fellow passengers might as well be dressed in stove pipe hats and beribboned lace! Time's functions are multifarious: time may heal; it also numbs, diminishes and etiolates. As such, time assumes many symbolic faces.

Was that, then, it? If time is both a sun and river, had it desiccated my feelings for my mother to a dribble of regret? Yes, the alchemy of memory being what it is, on reflection, I glossed with gold such fleeting happinesses as I could recall under mother's variously holed and leaking roofs; but in reality, after a life of extremes, of drug-induced abuse and abusive step-fathers, I couldn't keep out the recollection of cold wind and rain, of unadulterated alternations of unhappiness and pain.

So mother! You have died. And I am coming to lay you to rest at last! Then let me take advantage of that unique perspective and look back one last time! That's the good thing about nostalgia: it's never too late to enjoy it.

∞

## 64 – The tar-pit of doubt

After Auckland Avenue, those last few months at the bank fell into a very strange tempo: a sort of rhythmless inertia. Every day I entered the bank's vestibule time slowed down; but this time not in a good way: no, time ground to a halt - and so did my mind. My day became a tar-pit into which, like some moribund mammoth, I had stumbled. I could not drag myself out of the cloying black treacle of my banal banking existence; could not put one foot in front of another through my day without the most colossal effort of will – and willpower has its limits.

Conversely, the event in Auckland Avenue had taken hold of me and was now the greater, indeed, the irrefutable reality. It spoke with utter clarity - and not just in the form of memory. The experience stayed with me, its spirit refused to depart from me – like the spirit of a benign possession.

Not that I didn't continue to have doubts about Auckland Avenue. O I doubted – I doubted for England! My doubts were spectacular: in nightmares and daydreams I replayed them visually again and again in my mind, like great goals on Doubt of the Day for Gary Lineker and Alan Shearer to analyse.

Even if I *had* had this experience, what was I supposed to do with it? Stand on a soap-box and battle with the lunch-box laughter in Hyde Park? (Lunch-boxes?) Be reasonable, man! Get a grip! This kind of experience is unusual and rare to say the least, and as such should be treated as a happy aberration – to be treasured in private, not pored over in public. Think about it: life goes on; there's money to be earned; food to be put on tables. You can still have such extraordinary experiences and incorporate them into ordinary life. Can't you…………………...............................................? No.

## 65 – The arrival of Pegasus

As Kate's pregnancy began to approach its term, and even though a sense of responsibility commanded me not to get carried away, that was exactly what happened. I could no longer repress the remembered vigour of Auckland Avenue's inspiration; could no longer clip the wings of its mythical flight of fancy; no longer pinion my personal Pegasus… and mythical winged horses are notoriously unmanageable in the hands of office workers.

This unruly beast, this Pegasus-memory I had to ride; this great, white-winged horse laughed at my attempts to stay small, to retain the perspective of a normal life, to be 'normal', to live a normal life.

How many times he had taken me on his back and recalled to mind the heights to which I'd flown in Auckland Avenue! Well, not me: that was the point: 'I' had flown precisely by disappearing; and thus unburdened, something far more powerful had taken off! And continued to fly!

In fact, whenever I tried to do the simplest things at work, making coffee, logging on to the computer, going for a pub lunch, Pegasus loudly neighed. 'What? You're seriously pretending that drinking in a club compares to drinking from a fountain on Mount Helicon? Do me a favour!' he inveighed. And he was right: alcohol seemed such a poor substitute for Auckland Avenue's inspiration.

Thus, shifting from the actual to the ethereal, the physical to the symbolic, my mind identified more and more with Pegasus' point of view: after all, office life seemed so manifestly mad. But a horse laughing? Not literally of course. Though I have to say, the neighing of horses can sound weirdly close to laughter.

## 66 - The timelessness of a Dickensian upbringing

*Back in Bristol for mother's funeral I catch a bus and, from the top deck, scan the streets where I once lurched, stumbled and fell from childhood into adolescence.* My inevitably maudlin contemplations are interrupted by a bunch of school kids cackling with laughter further down the aisle. All laughter comprises an animalistic element. Indeed, laughter, when obviously inappropriate, betrays its weird bestial origins.

And mother often laughed inappropriately – the effect of the junk, I guess. I remember mother laughed right after she hit me one time. I was sixteen or so, and she had slapped me so hard in a row that it broke my nose. I remember coldly turning on her and saying:

'That's the last time you'll ever hit me...' And then I left. For good.

If it sounds melodramatic then let me not disown the violin; if the plot begins to sound Victorian, then let me freely admit my admiration for the essential timelessness of history and for beloved British stereotypes. Aren't we all, to some extent – whether rich man, poor man, beggar man or thief; banker, journalist and clerk, philanthropist and murderer, average or eccentric - eternally Dickensian?

And so it was that time that, with broken nose, I had set out on the road to my paternal grandparents in Hertfordshire (to this day I have always liked the way that county had the word 'heart' in it). They it was who took me in with all the Dickensian generosity we have come to know from Betsy Trotwood and Mr Dick.

Just say, then, that for two years until I left school, and having ambivalently left my mother to her destructive dependency, I experienced under my grandparents' roof that great unsung, secret, golden element of human nature – consistency.

'Consistency.' The word contains such a soft and simple sibilance smoothing such a rough and rasping challenge: to be equal-minded, level-headed and even-tempered to others, despite the pitch and roll, the stormy vicissitudes of one's own internal seas. Consistency: that quality that declares 'whatever my own circumstances I will always greet you according to my regard for you;

will always address myself to the current matter of our friendship, rather than use you to redress the deficiencies of my own mood. I will never, in other words, use you as a whipping-boy or girl; never abuse the principle of friendship as a convenient vent for my own spleen....'

I have, of course, just described my mother's attitude to her children. They – we, my sister and I - were sitting targets for her schizophrenic moods. She used to fire off shots at us according to her demonic playground whim; and our ducks rose and fell with tragicomic regularity. Her prize was the next fix.

Conversely, my grandparents were a revelation to me; indeed, went out of their way, perhaps, to compensate for the treatment they knew I had received at the hands, not just of my mother but of their own son, my quondam father....

'Your mother's not in her perfect mind,' declared my grandmother, Shakespeareanly understating the issue somewhat, as I intuited even then.

'She doesn't mean to hurt you.' - No? God knows what she'd do if she did, I thought.

'Don't you worry, we won't let anyone take you away again,' reassured my grandfather, Mr Dick.

And so what if my grandparents read like a translation from the time-blurred pages of a nineteenth century novel? I loved them. They drank tea from china cups, put

130

the milk in after the tea, actually ate tasteless cucumber sandwiches. In all their trivial habits they were admirable escapees from the annals of modern angst. Yes, I suppose what I liked best was precisely that they *were* identifiably old-fashioned. But aren't all grandparents? Aren't they supposed to be? Isn't being cut off from time precisely what we want from them: the unchanging certainty of a past our neurotic urgency cannot intrude upon, a bedrock no vicissitude or vogue can shake; a constant, a given, a reality underlying our own shifting sands – like the beauty of an ancient city discovered beneath the desert of our own? To a child, grandparents are more than a reassurance; they are the living proof of our potential victory over time and circumstance.

In this way, my own grandparents' consistency was a tacit promise actually to always be the same; to present a house with four walls and a roof both actually and metaphorically: the crockery ordered on the dresser; to say 'this is the way in, this is how we do things inside and this is the way out; none of this will ever change. This geography is secure. Its landscape is eternal.' The lost heart needs that kind of definite topography in order to locate its own co-ordinates at certain stages in life.

Anyhow, my grandparents do not come to my mother's funeral – principally because they, too, are dead. But standing by her grave focuses my feelings: I miss them more than her. Is this not a terrible admission? Yes, and no. At the death of one's parents one is allowed the luxury of private ambivalence. There are all the muted smiles and condolences, of course – well, not that many because mother's funeral is, as you might expect, sparsely attended: no-one loses friends as spectacularly efficiently over time as a junkie. But, of course, there is my sister, Cara. 'Dear one' her name means – though she had never felt dear – certainly not to mother.

We sit and talk over a coffee after the funeral. The rhythm between us is no more fluent than might be expected. In reminiscence, we smile at some of the right moments, and miss the beat at others. On taking leave of each other we exchange a melancholy glance in the tacit knowledge that there has been too much pain – and that our mutual secret would prevent us seeing each other much again...

∞

## 67 – Absurdity as an acid

Pegasus would never be broken in - that much was now clear to me. As the memorable sensation of what had befallen me in Auckland Avenue, my great white horse began to unseat me frequently during the day.

Whenever I went into the bank, whether to make that important call, finalise that deal, that trade – everything I did seemed set at one remove from reality; seemed, indeed, almost cinematically unreal; seemed, in fact, like entering a cinema: high-streets, pubs and bars, restaurants - especially cinemas! - all thus acquired the ambiguous folly of cinema. Cinema! - with its vital, prerequisite denial of all that's close to home! Its truth projected out there in the darkened distance! Even my conscience seemed like a remote, celluloid contrivance; seemed, in fact, like a cinema. Cinema with its seductive sequences of images and moods! Cinema, at once so real and so false! I remember an advert that used to say 'Life is your movie' – the ad men didn't know how right they were. - And yet... somehow, in every scene I took part in: the cinematic train to work, the doctor's surgery, the country walk, the 'take' was always ruined by the appearance of a white horse standing somewhere on the fringes of the set.

### 68 – A worsening of symptoms

*Back at the depot after the funeral, back behind the wheel of the bus, a routine anxiety kicks in. This is substantiated by my bereavement: my mind is undergoing a very definite period of readjustment - what with mother being dead and all.* But on the bus I can't hear myself think.

'Don't relax! The moment you relax is the moment you crash the bus!' Big Len's warning echoes in my memory... and finds a bodily echo in my increasingly dyspeptic stomach and further down my alimentary canal. My trips to the loo are now frequent – too frequent.

And now there's blood in it. Blood that I last saw flowing untimely from a young man's leg is now making an appearance in my stools.

Blood! Amorphous, viscous liquid… it's so obviously meant to stay inside you, yet it seeps out like a red, protean ghost to let you know you are on the verge of seriously changing shape – you, you unwilling human shape-shifter, as ultimately indeterminate as the spreading blood that leaks from cuts, abrasions, wounds, various parts of the body, noses, vaginas, penises – and in this case, and with a predictably attendant indignity, my arse. Nor does the fact that I'll be working nights for a few weeks fill me with optimism.

## 69 – Bodily effluents

*Back behind the wheel of my bus at night, the cast in the human drama changes; as a director I have to do the best with what I'm offered. And the later it gets the drossier my characters on board my bus become…* drunkards, hooligans, nutcases, I take them in my stride, push them this way and that across London's stage. Not that I trust them to perform as they should - not for a minute – the stabbing has changed all that. No, you, my passengers, as midnight approaches, might take things into your own hands and extemporise at any moment – especially when drunk. Take this pair of jokers stamping around above my head upstairs.

There are no lavatories on a bus – not unless you include pissing on my head from the seats upstairs. This seems to be an acceptable option for the drunken kids who have lurched into the seats directly above me. The first trickles of urine appear as beady-eyed rivulets of amber materialising out of the formica walls of my cabin.

Its then I know we are in for a rainy night. I can stop the bus, go upstairs, object, attempt to throw off the offenders and possibly be stabbed for my pains... or I can put up with it and mop up the piss with something from my bag of last resort. I do the latter. I am afraid the months have taken their toll on my sense of umbrage. It - the piss – is now all part of the night's work in this capital of drunkenness.

Puke, however – and howsoever delivered - is different.

I can hardly blame the young: I myself remember how compulsory it was to vomit up one's drink at a certain age. Not planned of course, but somehow unconsciously agreed upon: I will drink 'til it is suddenly too late to stop, 'til I can no longer stand, 'til my body can no longer stand what's inside of me. Then it will come back out... on this bus.... My bus.

I can hear it now happening down the aisle of my bus. The celebrated call for those old friends    Hughie and Ruth! I stop my bus.

'Hughieeeeeeee! Ruuuuth!' cries out a vomiting young woman, surrounded by two consolatory friends.

'Look, you'd better get her home.' I tell them. The puking girl calls out again for her old friends.

'Hughieeeeeeee! Ruuuuth!' Again, Hughie and Ruth refuse to come to her aid.

'We're tryin' ter get 'ome now!' caterwauls her friend. 'Why else d'yer think we're on a fuckin' bus?'

'Please don't use that language. I'm going to have to ask you to get her off.'

'What d'yer mean? 'Ow else are we gonna get 'er 'ome?'

'Get a taxi. Call her dad ---'

'She hasn't got a dad – not one she can telephone anyway…' scowls the friend.

'Hughieeeeeeee! Ruuuuth!' calls out the puking girl again, in despair.

'Not my problem, I'm afraid. Now I'm not moving the bus until you get her off.' Grudgingly the girls descend amidst much effing and blinding. As they depart I turn to take stock of the olfactory damage.

I've learned to take most things, but vomit is a problem. Forget the ugliness of the body's physical efforts to effect the act of vomiting – the distended jaw and creased, reticulated face; the abreactive stomach, the distorted groans, the grotesque moans - all unified in a repulsive, inverse parody of sexual delight; forget the whole massive, spiritual contortion necessary to harness the power to disgorge the contents of one's craw – forget these, I say – and focus not even on the unseemly, vivid, ochre bile, unlike any colour seen this side of hell – but focus, instead, upon that unmistaken nightmare smell...

The stink of puke is eternal. Related to, but infinitely worse than, chips eaten in the car, the stench of sick, once admitted to your intimate environment, is with you for life. Like an ingenuous evil spirit negligently discharged from hell, puke suddenly pops up beside you on the seat and says 'hello, I know you well!'

From that day on, puke invades your sense of smell; wherever you may go, like a nursery rhyme persona, leave her alone and little Bo Puke's sheep are sure to find you. In cars, kitchens, lavatories and dining-rooms; on clothes, carpets and pavements, the spirit of puke lingers long after the ghosts of all other experiences have gone home to their rightful resting-places.

The bus is no different. Indeed, it is my experience that, once puked-upon, no bus ever recovers from the olfactory shame. Better to scrap the bus – but, no, somehow the bus company don't see it that way. Disinfectant? You might as well try and disinfect your soul after committing murder. It just won't wash. Ask Lady Macbeth.

The puker doesn't care, of course; he or she's long ago been hustled and jumbled off the bus by mates slightly less drunk than him, leaving you, and the rest of the passengers to get on with it – and you do. You drive on just the same into the darkness...the darkness, that covers people's self-awareness in a shroud of false privacy. False because it doesn't conceal certain acts of intimacy. Take these two going at it upstairs at the back...

## 70 – Up Periscope!

*Up periscope! Sort of. My cabin periscope is precisely that: a simple, primary-school affair of angled mirrors situated up and to the right of my line of vision.* Peering into it at precise moments I can get a glimpse of the size and restrainability of any offenders upstairs; who's roughly doing what, and how, to whom – and whether I should be letting – or am physically able to stop - them do it. With couples canoodling this can turn me into an unwilling voyeur. I generally put up with it, so long as it doesn't straddle chairs or fellow travellers' communal sense of umbrage - but the full Monty; well that's another kettle of randy fish, and not to sound like a Brighton Boarding-house landlady from a Pinter play, but I can't let that go on: I have my clientele's morals to consider! Besides which intense foreplay above one's ahead is distracting to the driver. I usually don't stop the bus unless they're physically or metaphorically rocking the boat. – Like this couple...

'Excuse me but I'm going to have to ask you to desist!' I say to the teenage couple in question. God knows why I used the word 'desist'! The Victorian in me, I suppose.

'Yer what?' asked the young man as his giggling girl friend covers her face.

'You'll have to stop.'

'Stop what? We weren't doing nuffing mate!'

Then suddenly overwhelmed by a loathing of double negatives I correct him in true schoolmasterly fashion: 'Then you *were* doing *something!*'

'What?'

'If you weren't doing nothing, you were doing something...'

'Fuck off! Jesus, come on Karen, this bloke's a fuckin' weirdo!'

And off they get, smirking, leaving me and one other pensioner to people our strangely purposeless, peaceful, un-erotic hell.

### 71 – Drinking the sweet red wine of loneliness

*And so, way past midnight, my bus drives right on through the heart of loneliness! As a bus-driver; past midnight I cruise the concourse of the city's lustful loneliness.* With the shows over and the restaurants empty, what is lonelier than being purposeless in the metropolis at night? The city mocks loneliness - but also encourages it. This makes nocturnal journeying a deeply ambivalent experience.

At night, buses offer accidental companionship. Around midnight that intimacy intensifies. Who has not shared, if not a secret love affair, then certainly an intense relationship with the only other traveller, last man or woman, on the bus at way past midnight? One slips in and out of consciousness of this intimacy as the minutes and dark roads slip by until finally at the point of break-up you feel a sublimated sense of abandonment as your partner in solitude steps out into the night leaving you all alone... except for me: I remain: custodian of companionability, I rescue you from the decay of your abandonment by closing the bus doors on night and accelerating away from its loneliness; accelerate only to deliver you to the more comfortable punishment of your home address, where, like Socrates, you willingly drink sleep's hemlock in an uncanny nightly impersonation and presentiment of your own death....

But after that, at dead of night, as you lie dreaming, I still have a bus to drive, a bus to get back to the depot on my own, with no one else on board apart from all the ghosts of those I've driven throughout the day.

Driving the empty bus back to the depot at night, with all your passengers dropped off in town is called 'running light' – and you do! Like Mercury, with winged shoes you grace the streets of London with your momentary presence and then are gone, leaving all the day's heaviness behind. And with it those poor fools standing at bus-stops who have not spotted your 'out of service' blinds until too late when you fly past them, one finger raised at their not uncomical anger and very temporary despair; your impotent vindictiveness forgivable, perhaps, only because you have had a day in hell and it was people like them who put you there.

The tables have turned; so, too, the planet's hemispheres, and with them the whole palette of experience: day's monochrome blossoms into hallucinogenic neon visions. The city is a trip at night. London sleeps like a dragon as you slip through the coils of its empty streets, traffic lights hung red, gold and green like lanterns signalling an escape route through a cinematic underworld: the lovers framed in half-lit doorways, the drunk serenading a sober, unresponsive moon, the prostrate vagrant and the biblical passer-by, the constable's soliloquy of calm upon the intercom - actors fluent in the cadences of darkness! And as these fluorescent lives flare neon-bright and die, so, too, the dragon's malevolence dissolves. For a moment you think 'why flee a creature whose sleep bespeaks so lyrical a labyrinth? Who is the courier that drives me from this dream? Whose hands are these upon the steering wheel?'

∞

## 72 – Pegasus galloping through the bank

Finally, one morning, a few months after Auckland Avenue I woke up in the flat with Pegasus' breath in my face. The great beast was standing by my bed, pawing at the carpet, plainly anxious to get me up and get on with something vital I had forgotten. What was it? Ah yes – a total change in my life's direction. At least Pegasus seemed to know which way to go.

That direction lay away from Kate – spiritually if not physically. I tried to take her with me, encouraged in discussions her to ride Pegasus with me – but Kate had never been keen on horses. She was even less keen on my resigning from the bank.

'Don't joke, Matt I'm not in the mood for it.'

'I'm not joking. I can't stand it anymore. I've *got* to leave…. Everything's changed.'

'You're damn right everything's changed: I'm seven months pregnant!'

'It'll be fine. We've got money in the bank ---'

'Which you're leaving! ---'

'We can live off it for a while ---'

'How long!?'

'Long enough, then I'll get something else – something menial - to pay the bills, I mean.'

'Matt, it's crazy – you're… I can't talk to you in this mood. I'm going out.'

We had this argument several times in different ways over the next week or so; sometimes sharply, personally, at others almost lazily, disinterestedly, as though it applied not to us but to some other theoretical couple. What it always came down to was the fact that the event in Auckland Avenue had been fatal, had mortally wounded my desire to make money, to get ahead, get on in life. Whatever I did henceforth would just be a holding exercise to earn cash to pay the bills – until I decided what I really wanted to do with the rest of my life.

'It's self-sabotage, Matt!' claimed Kate, desperately: 'You're just frightened of success! What it *means*!'

'All right! What *does* it mean? You tell me!' I demanded rhetorically. 'Driving myself mad talking to morons about money all day? Getting arseholed in clubs with Ronnie? Standing around at stupid dinners with stupid punters and their stupid wives! That's what it means!'

And so we debated the concept of success like two people banging their heads against opposite sides of the same wall; because actually I felt I *was* successful, as it happens; felt that, in its way, and on its own highly uncommercial terms, the event in Auckland Avenue, with its sublime unity, its utter emotional and psychological release, did indeed represent a kind of absolute success. No, Kate was wrong: it wasn't about a fear of success: we all want to succeed; wise men who reject the world to meditate in caves, saints who long for union with their, for me, bizarre version of god, want success – and so did I – just not the sort of success the bank's values represented. That sort of success now seemed to me... well – unsuccessful.

### 73 – Shift-work

*And so my life on board the bus constantly shifts – the whole axis of my world shifts from day to night and night back to day, according to the shift I'm on.* Day becomes night and I sleep with the curtains closed; night becomes day and I wake with the lights full on at midnight. Yes, it shifts: not only day becomes night, but wrong becomes right. Anything goes. I certainly do. With increasing regularity.

The fact appals me: I have been driving now for nearly a year, and in response to my departure from the rhythms of the circadian clock my 'illness' has now progressed down the line in seriousness – from the suburbs of acceptable discomfort to its Waterloo of outright pain. What began as an occasional stomach-ache, is thus now visiting me with prolonged cramps; is, in effect, like an ugly creditor leaving the calling-card of serious intent. I avoid it – and him - by darting in and out of the shadows of my own existence, the night-shift and day-shift axis of my world. How much longer I can conduct this fugitive existence is not clear; there is, after all, only so much energy one can usefully devote to fleeing from one's own body before the latter gets tired of the game of hide and seek and calls the game abruptly to a halt.

For, evidently, my body now has a life of its own. It dines when it wants; gives no warning when it wants to shit or piss; gets exhausted and bails on me at a moment's notice. No, my body self-evidently no longer does what I tell it to. It's like a rebellious daughter: on night shifts, when my mind is asleep, my body stays out late on its own, hangs out with strange types. And then, back on day-shift again, when my mind wakes up, when normal people are getting up, my body drifts off to sleep; if I stir it, it resents me deeply; it reacts badly to the simplest requests from me: my head aches and my stomach is prone to sudden outbursts. There's no denying it, my body and me are not on the best of terms at the moment, but I'm hoping it's just a phase she's going through; hoping she'll grow out of it.

Maybe that's it: maybe it is growing out of me; maybe I'm experiencing the growing pains of a body growing out of the mind of the person embodied in it. Isn't that a definition of cancer? The growth of an autonomous function within the host body, one that takes over and diverts all vital functions away from the body to itself? Maybe my body is taking me over. My stomach creases me up twice a day at the moment. An ulcer? Cancer? The pain is so sharp, I nearly cry out.

∞

## 74 – Swing-doors

The day – no, the *instant* I left the bank it forgot me in a heartbeat. Such was her loyalty to our love affair that in

145

the blink of an eye the Old Lady of Threadneedle Street denied my very existence.

There's something simultaneously exciting and unfulfilling about exiting from swing doors: their continuous motion both sweeps you out and denies you closure at the same time. I remember turning round and looking back at them and the bank's chic vestibule to make sure I'd left.

I had.

There is nothing so irremediably closed to us as a memory that has disowned us.

## 75 - Womankind

Did I ever think of leaving Kate? Of course. Would it have been the most despicable act of my life? Certainly. Maybe, even pregnant as she was, Kate thought of leaving me? It was impossible to say what she felt at times.

But then, what had I done to deserve disclosure of the precise geography and general whereabouts of Kate's love, other than become, as I've alluded, gradually more distant myself? At times, over those first few months following the revelation of Kate's pregnancy, our love-making had alternated between superb perfunctoriness and strangely desperate enjoyment. Then after a couple of months we had stopped making love: it seemed natural – to stop, I mean; there being so obviously three people involved in the intensely Oedipal arrangement.

So, distance was the context we had begun to operate in. After a while it supplied all our proportions. And with distance came the perspective of an almost amused indifference. We mutually saw each other down the wrong ends of a telescope: simultaneously small and yet distinct; indeed, oddly iconic: there-but-not-there, almost mythically optional in each other's eyes. I was thus Orpheus calling out to an increasingly remote Eurydice. Half the time Kate-Eurydice didn't know whether to ignore me or run back to me – and when she did I barely recognised her; didn't know whether to kiss or question her identity! But then women have always been a mystery to me.

Womankind: what to say upon the subject that hasn't been said a thousand times more felicitously by minds more clear-sighted than mine? What to see and how, indeed, to describe it with my myopic vision? For, my own mother apart – a woman, I should say, un-womaned by drugs - women's power blinds me.

What! Do you have the unreconstructed temerity to call woman a 'subject?' What clearer indictment of bare-faced chauvinism, of the aggressively objectifying male gaze could be required? 'We find you guilty! Guilty as charged before you open your mouth further!'

Puts black cap on.

'You shall be taken from this page to a place of radical feminist execution where you shall be hanged by the neck until... until... what? Dead?

So be it. Can't the dead still speak? Don't ghosts haunt us in the ghoulish tones of conscience? Then let me hold forth in their language! The outlawed dialect of the male of the species, the expletive-littered lyric of his basic phallic nature! The risen cock of the letter 'I'! in our flattened alphabet! The desperate grunt of the male chauvinist pig in our modern sanitised sty.

'Madam! The convict in the dock, allowed one last statement, addresses you! What have you to say?

'Woman...'

'Go on, speak up, man!

'This, my lady.... Now that you, yourself, stand exonerated by the age - innocent of every charge upon which history formerly indicted you – how should we, the new second sex, address you? With what language should we speak, if our dialect is self-evidently too rude, too crude for public use? For in our need for you we stand recidivist - defeated; indeed, our very need for you will always be profoundly primitive. Our manners may be re-shaped, but the beast's blood is more ancient than Stonehenge; again, its river may be diverted – but only underground, where neither men nor women can drink from it, or be revitalised thereby....

I had had this discussion with Kate after she and I had endured one of our stand-up rows with mother: afterwards Kate objected to my penchant for poetry in cases of simple sexual polity.

'You put women on a pedestal precisely because your mother is a bitch!' she had a point.

'But we don't want your worship. It's bad for both of us.'

I conceded the danger here was, of course, a romantic tendency to idealise and thus to miss the modern woman behind the classical disguise. That said, when it comes to sex and sexuality, dare we gloss over the dark recidivism that flows in all our veins? Where desire and need are concerned are we, in fact, dealing with forces under sociological control? Am I exclusively a social construct? Or are we the hopeful victims of our own hoax: the politics of sexual equality? Need equality mean sameness?

'What? Of course, men and women are the same! What makes them any different?' implored Kate.

'Nothing – except for everything,' I replied, playing the absolutist hand. We agreed to differ – and did not make love that night.

Sometimes I think I must be mad; must be missing something obvious; at others it all seems so obvious to me. Men and women the same? Really..?

We moderns pride ourselves on our freedom from mythic prejudice, but is it precisely our lust for objectivity that enabled such a monstrously false equivalence to pass the test of modern sensibility? Is the demand for objectivity itself not just one more prejudice when the subjective facts stare us in the face so obviously? And why do we fear the implications of our differences? Why should 'difference' imply inferiority? Do those who convince themselves it does, really only betray their need to mask their own mediocrity by parading under the flag of equality? Is it in answer to such questions that the French – nation of lovers – came up with the great response: 'vive la difference!'

Woman! So manifestly and manifoldly different from the male! Your body so full of secrets, a cavernous landscape of sudden light and dark, of suns and moons that dawn and set in their own private interior. Woman! Sphinx-like spirit that retreats to her own heartland as mysteriously as she advances from it towards us – to kill or cure? To kiss or cut us in two?

Woman who, as the mysterious, omnipotent purveyor of so much pleasure, be it psychological, physical or spiritual, cannot but achieve a goddess-like status in the eyes of men.

You say you don't want our worship, but need divinity be so onerous; need it mean only Victorian purity? Didn't the Greeks get it right again: their poets, I mean, not their idiotic pseudo-democrats - when they named so many different goddesses and gave them Shakespearean infinite variety?

Woman, multi-faceted, Hydra-headed shape-shifting persona: in the gallery of human statuary, the terrible truth is that, for man, your pedestal is not optional – and yet you, more than man, may choose your form! Your faces range from Goddess of love and beauty, Aphrodite, through Athena and Artemis, hunters of wisdom's form and Imagination's moony moods, to the Gorgon's mask of death, via scores of others in between. Woman, you may confirm man with a glance or kill him with a deathly stare - even then, was not Medusa strangely beautiful? Did not the snakes perform a hypnotic ballet in her hair?

Woman, to whom we men owe our very life! Your breast the fountain whence we drink of life; your smell the first we know of flowers and of perfume; your lap and hips the first we know of any landscape we might inhabit without threat. And so you cradle us and nourish our strength even as yours diminishes. Why *are* men stronger if not to gain the strength to make the vital leap away from you; leap the bounds of your overwhelming influence and thus stake out our own ground...? Woman, both in and through time, so ancient and so modern: your timelessness is thus your blessing and your curse; your body, our cradle and our hearse.

Woman... we never can forgive you for your power.

Woman.... Your punishment is the prison of our love.

## 76 – Piped music in the bus

*Something has to change! It's not just the stabbing, puking and screwing on the bus that has worsened my colonic experiences, it is the constant raised levels of anxiety day-in, day-out.* I am now desperate to improve an un-improvable situation, I begin to resort to the realms of fantasy for support. I decide music is needed. Music will calm me down, calm my passengers – calm the world down!

'I'm not putting up with it, not any more!' I announce to Kate.

'Not putting up with what?'

'The bus. The whole environment stinks. The way people have to travel. It must be possible to change it; at least change the conditions.'

'And how are you going to do that?' whispers the voice of doubt.

'Make the goddam journey more pleasant. People need peace. – I thought a bit of music!' This is how mad I have become.

'Music?'

'Ambient music… Eno. Whatever. Pleasant sounds. It must be possible to make the whole experience less… mediocritising…'

'Surely travelling by bus is meant to be shitty.'

Now I detest piped music as much as, if not more than, the next man; that said, there's music and music. The sort of music I plan to pipe into my passengers' minds has the virtue of being as unprescriptive as possible. I shall not force them to be happy; there will be no words for a start, no lyrics, no love songs, no confected ecstasy or heartbreak - only a musical catharsis on a very subtle, almost subliminal level. The sounds will be so soft as to be almost inaudible. I say, almost... Obviously I want them to hear it. I want to hear it, for chrissake. Anything that makes me and my passengers feel even vaguely alive on the way to work has got to be a good thing, hasn't it?

Needless to say, the innovation to set up a small stereo in my bus is mad – and illegal; indeed, any minute alteration of the bus's basic working functions is profoundly prohibited. But it's too late: I now have the wind under my tail and the spirit of a very minor devilry riding in me. Having researched my purchase with the due diligence of the pathologically optimistic, I then buy a small, reasonably affordable portable, multi-speaker sound system offering wireless connection between amp and speakers. I also buy Blue-tac.

On the planned morning, I transport said sound system concealed into the bus and rig everything into place. A few minutes go by and suddenly I am welcoming my first passengers on board. Eno's 'Thursday Afternoon' was my chosen subliminal anthem for the doomed. Played so softly I hoped they'd hardly notice that it was, in fact, Friday morning. Sadly one did.

'Not sure I like that, driver!'

'What, the music, madam?'

'Call it that if you like. Sounds like a headache.'

'Well, I hope it soothes any headaches on board!' I reply limply.

The woman sort of snorts and proceeds down the bus. I see a couple of teenagers look up from their seats, as if double-taking at something heavenly they've heard; but they reassure themselves by blanking it out with their own headphones. An old style businessman looks around, then somewhat irritably opens The Times with as much fractured crispness as possible, knocking over the handbag of the young woman next to him. He picks it up graciously, but then declares loudly:

'I do apologise. Just that one can't hear oneself think in here!'

'Oh I don't know – it's rather nice,' she replies in my defence.

But this is not going well. The rest of the passengers are too locked into their own mental diaries to fit in Eno's subliminal celebration of 'Thursday Afternoon'.

And those few that are, are seemingly not fond of Thursdays.

∞

## 77 – Birth of a statue

The birth of our son is not easy. He resists passing through the doorway opened by his poor mother's labour and takes 27 hours to be delivered – almost as if he has had second thoughts about the wisdom of being reborn to this human life. Who could blame him?

But it is too late for any such hesitations. Here he is: bold as brass in his mother's arms. Not so much brass, as alabaster. In fact, he has the quality of a statuette, not entirely of this world, yet somehow related to it in some ideal way I cannot put my finger on. Indeed, such is the porcelain fragility of his humanity that I fear to place my hands upon him at all.

'Take him', encourages Kate. I do so.

From such small beginnings do such monumental joys and sorrows grow. Right now he is silent as stone, offering up none of the neonate's proverbial wailing. The midwife reassures us somewhat prosaically that this is not evidence of his precociously meditative sensibility, but is rather the result of shock from the trials of labour.

Whatever its source, he gazes out with a singularity and quietude I cannot help but hope will remain part of his temperament throughout his life. I show him the outside world through the hospital window. Of course he cannot see it, his new-born eyesight capacity being no further than a foot or so (for most of us this never changes). So I behold the sight for him and wonder at what awaits him out there.

'Look Tom – the world.' I say. But Tom just looks up at me, as if rapt by the sight of the second strange inhabitant of that self-same alien world he has come back to visit. For is there not something strangely familiar about its perfumes and softnessneses, its hard edges, its light and shade, its sense of movement and sudden stillness? Who is this strange man - and this strange woman? Why do they think they know me?

### 78 - Platonic dialogue with Clever Clive

*My piped music experiment has not gone well; but then music is so personal: one man's Mozart is another man's muzak. Back at the depot, Clever Clive points this out to me.*

'We've 'ad a complaint. I'm sure you know what it's about…'

One short bus-ride was all it had taken; one short three-penny jaunt for some miserable tone-deaf son-of-a-bitch to report that Eno's ambient music had not, in fact, been played subliminally enough upon my bus; doubtless interrupting their silent meditation on Fermat's last theorem.

Clever Clive was a decent enough guy about it: sat there on his battered office-world throne, a cardinal of the timetable, a primate of punctuality and time and motion orthodoxy, he calmly conducted a low-key, man-to-man inquisition into both my heterodoxy and the details of the travelling customer's treacherous denunciation.

'May I ask what the fuck you think you're doing? - No, actually, 'old it right there! - 'cos I couldn't give a monkey's arse what you think you're doing. You're on your second verbal warning, all right?'

'What, for playing a bit of music ---'

'Yes, "for playing a bit of music!" Are you fucking mental? Don't answer that because I know the answer! Never 'eard anything like it – and nor 'ave our customers, I shouldn't wonder..! Just sign here...'

With a silent swirl of the biro I acknowledge the fact of our meeting and that I would receive confirmation of the conclusions thereof in the post within one working week.

And of course Clever Clive was right. As I pushed the signed document back to him across the desk, he went into greater detail about his reasons for the official warning.

'You see, as I say, Matt, music is so personal! – May I call you Matt?' He'd been calling me Matt for weeks.

'Yes, Matt, I'm sure you'd agree, being a sensitive soul, that music has, above all, the power to restore that which was lost. Music is vicarious emotion transplanted into your heart, thus reviving you when you've previously been lost in a Persistent Vegetative State!

'But Matt, some people don't wish to be unconditionally revived from mortal torpor - like a Frankenstein monster into a world of someone else's emotion – which is what music is: exchanging your lack of feeling for someone else's – because music is thus also an admission that our emotional identity is, again, a lot more fluid than we care to think.'

Clever Clive hardly pauses for breath before continuing his Platonic dialogue:

'To picture myself as a CD player for a moment, Matt: if I can eject the emotion I'm feeling and replace it with, say, some dead composer's, aren't I saying his feelings are better than my own? Some people just don't want that kind of experience on a bus! – Not to mention stealing someone else's emotions – what about authenticity, Matt?'

I'm not prepared to let this go. Clive is labouring under a delusion about the nature of identity.

'But that assumes it _is_ stealing, Clive! – May I call you Clive? The fact is it's not stealing, it's sharing the composer's emotions. He's not wandering around with an empty heart – he's already dead: that's my point!

158

'In reliving his emotion we sort of clone the dead composer back into existence? If I literally become the emotions I experience, don't I to that extent restore him to life?'

Clever Clive sits back and ponders this. I push home my point.

'Don't all artists literally live again in this way when we revel in their work? If we are really no more than the vividness of our feelings, both acted out or simply experienced, is there such a thing as death?

These are a few of the things that Clever Clive and I don't discuss at the depot as I receive my official warning – and then rush straight to the loo – for the third time that day.

∞

## 79 – Afterwards

Following our son Tom's birth, our flat had thus become a strange menagerie, sheltering a first-born, his exhausted mother, me – and a great white horse - since Pegasus was now stabled with us too. It is hard to keep a horse in a small London flat. Pegasus, great wind-horse of inspiration! Could you not, divine beast, see how inconvenient your presence was?

Ah but what do the gods and their divine entourage care about trivial mortal domestic arrangements? Once you invite them into your house you must expect them to take centre stage – yes, even if you've just had a baby. The baby needs the breast: give it that and forget the rest! Stand aside! Pegasus - sired by Poseidon, foaled by Medusa – requires space!

Indeed, one can only repress the power of a seminal experience for so long until it demands expression, and I had suppressed all that Pegasus stood for, close-confined this equine spirit of inspiration beyond his bounds of patience. He needed to gallop. He needed the wind in his mane. For this I couldn't blame him. Nor could I blame Kate – exhausted, constantly breast-feeding - for tiring of a horse parading around in her bedroom; but what else to do with the damned animal?

Anyway, one morning I must have come down with a certain look in my eye, like that of one of Stubb's horses being attacked by a lion – and Kate knew something was terminally awry.

'Are you all right..?

'Mm?' I barely raised my head.

'For chrissake, stop being so fucking distant…!'

Distant? Me? Yes - as distant as Neptune is from Neasden. Neither love nor sound carry across such distances. I said nothing during breakfast and nothing as I washed up – and then nothing as Kate smashed the cup of coffee I passed her. Cue for Tom to wake up and cry.

That sound – that sound that is the most accusative sound in human experience!

## 80 - Bad Reputation

*The worse my colonic situation becomes the more desperate I am to contain it.* I begin to plan my timetable and my route around where I can stop, get out and quickly evacuate my bowels - pubs, public loos, etc. And I also carry with me into my cabin every day a vital bag of personal toiletry effects. This I call my aforementioned 'bag of last resort' – a euphemism from banking days which I tritely indulge in. Trouble is, the other drivers cannot fail to observe how close is my comparative cleanliness to their implied un-godliness – and to take offence.

'Ere 'e comes! Big Jessie with 'is bag of tricks! Wot've you got for us today? Bit of Chanel Number One?! Be a dear: dab some behind me 'ear-holes!'

Their jests fall on deaf ears - just as my arse falls on their damp seats.

When you get into a bus driver's seat, don't think it's fresh and new each day – it's rank with cold sweat, the chill and smelly aftermath of another body's exertions at the wheel – and the wheel itself is clammy and smeared by the dodgy, podgy fingers of another driver's feel – or lack of feel – for life. The cheap plastic vaguely stinks of yesterday's mildew; a residue of breath and farts hangs in the air. The bus cabin is repulsive with the stain of human mediocrity.

Clean it! Yes, go OCD on it if you must, but do not go gentle into that good bus! Clean everything around you! With sprays, perfumes, disinfectants, alcohol solutions – cloths – can't have too many cloths! Cloths to wipe and cloths to wash! Cloths to cleanse away the dross!

And a towel.

A towel to drape over the driver's seat and disguise the fact and feel of another driver's arse and thighs. It isn't perfect of course; life suffers from seepage; repel it as we may, that which is undesired always seeps through in the end. But the towel does at least delay the inevitable until later in the day, back at the depot. There, another daily problem is encountered.

If the toilets are empty then all is well and good; but if they are not... if they are not.... Of course, it has to happen: this one time I am forced into the ladies' loo; what else can I do with all doors closed to me; the men's, shut for repairs; the manager's, for cleaning.

Women are cleaner than men. Mostly. Because they have to sit, women's aim is sure in all they do: their urine hits the target, so, too, does their somehow more fragrant and more shapely poo. Still, as a man, however desperate your need, you feel furtive in the ladies' loo; like some kind of pervert. Please god don't let anyone come; don't let them see it's you.

'What the fuck are you doin'?' - Having finished, I open the loo door straight into Donna's face.

'No, don't tell me: I'm sure you've got a great reason. Tell me later – in the women's showers! I follow Donna's encouragement... and flee down the corridor into the spider's web of night – and an increasingly unhappy marriage.

∞

## 81 – Beyond the human pale

I had pushed Kate beyond the pale. She was exhausted by weeks of broken sleep and breastfeeding – and now I had both abandoned our means of income - and unconsciously entered a Trappist monastery.

'Look, I can't bear any more of this – tell me what's wrong!'

As I said, she would have been mad not to think me mad. In one respect: if the treadmill of banal routine is sanity, then actually I *was* mad: had I not felt violently compelled by some force greater than myself to get off it. But "some force greater than myself..."? Surely, this ludicrous phrase augurs badly where other people's credulity is concerned. Are we even allowed to use such an expression these days? Can there be any force greater than ourselves that doesn't raise the dogmatic hackles of our materialistic disbelief? God is after all, long dead, as Nietzsche declared. Furthermore, 'the death of one god is the death of all', as the poet Wallace Stevens further averred.

So what do I mean by 'some force greater than myself'? Certainly, I'm not talking about anything religious. I don't mean god as some bearded geezer poncing around on clouds; or any less naïve conception of some transcendent power; I don't mean the 'ground of being' itself, and I certainly don't mean voices in my head. I don't mean anything external to myself – or lack of self... what I mean is....

'Look, why don't you see someone?' Kate suddenly suggests.

'See someone?'

'It's not normal – it can't be normal.'

'What? You mean a shrink... I don't think so,' I said dismissively – and then realised how appropriate the term was. In truth, a shrink was exactly what one desperate part of me needed – but only if he could do what his medicine said on the box – shrink my world back to normal, to manageable proportions. Because the event in Auckland Avenue didn't have any proportions. That was its problem: it was a proportion-less experience – when you, yourself, turn into the sun you tend to lose interest in your 'to-do' list; I mean the diary dates are still there, you know you've got a singing lesson to go to, but it can wait whilst you illuminate the South of England.

No, Kate was right. I was definitely not normal…

That word again: 'Normal'.

'Normal': that beloved state of mind to which a part of me was suddenly, deeply, lustfully attracted; 'normal', the 36-24-36 inch world where I had a name I recognised, a job that kept me off the streets (literally), a life that made at least a little sense…. Yes, Pegasus my arse! To hell with horses – mythical or metaphorical! I had one last chance and its name was 'Normal'! I had fallen in love with 'normalcy'. She was suddenly the only girl for me and I must claim her for my own.

### 82 – Finally, the doctor

*So Kate has forced me to see a consultant about my troubled bowels and here he is - the consultant - sticking his finger up my bottom for reasons not entirely clear to me - unalloyed perversity perhaps. Then he registers me for imminent exploratory tests down the corridor.* My prostate seems fine, he reassures me; but still, he goes on, it'd be nice to know what we're dealing with, if anything.

Indeed, it would. I'm not good with physical pain. Mental pain I'm OK with. I mean, I don't like it but I can deal with it, come to terms with it, so to speak. Indeed, we speak the same language, me and mental pain: we know where we're coming from. We may not always agree but essentially we're singing from the same Presbyterian, protestant, puritanical song-sheet: guilt.

And this we can discuss, bargain over; at least work out a viable relationship on the basis of which we can each get through the day.

But bodily pain: that's quite a different matter. I once said to Kate, only half-jokingly, that you could define woman as that half of the human race who bear unbelievable pain with great fortitude - childbirth being the prime example – but who, when they stub their toe or prick a finger on a pin, bring the house down with wails of grief drawn from some abyss of agony only inhabited by unclassified monsters of the unconscious.

Anyway, I do the hospital tests, which are, of course, inconclusive, off the record containing one slightly raised protein level, but nothing to suggest that cancer has set in or is imminently like to do.

'Am I perhaps under any strain I can think of? Any stress?' inquires the only half-engaged consultant (I am, after all, only one of the scores of patients whose death warrants he will sign or tear up this week).

Any stress? Now let me see.....

Aaaaaaarghhh! I scream violently at the consultant. He is shocked into an immediate cardiac arrest and dies on the spot – which translates as 'no...no more than usual.... I mean I've had a change of job: I used to work in an investment bank and now I drive a bus - and a few months ago I had a visionary experience which destroyed my faith in things as they are, resulting in an existential crisis. But apart from that, no, nothing I can think of...'

'Well, we'll obviously keep the situation monitored. Come back in a month's time and we'll do some more tests. Until then, make sure you're getting your usual five-a-day,' he consoles me.

Five-a-day, eh? Five what? Five sessions of peacefully ecstatic meditation; of sexual delight with a Hollywood starlet; of laps round Monaco with Lewis Hamilton? No, five-a-day means five fruit-and-veg to you, mate. For you are of the suburbs. Normal is your name and normal is your game.

That said, strangely, 'normal' has an air of ecstasy about it when you depart from the shadow of a hospital. Suddenly 'normal; is no longer just 'normal; suddenly 'normal' is an oxygenised revelation – an abnormal happening - a miracle; suddenly, without warning, 'normal' is the miracle you've been searching for all your life – and all the time it was right in front of you. (But I still need to go to the loo again.)

∞

## 83 – Shrink.

So the shrink looks at me and asks me about Auckland Avenue:

'Now, Matt, describe to me again what it feels like? What happens in these.... events?' - as if they were like Wimbledon or Hickstead: delightful social occasions experienced through a haze of strawberries and cream – against which paradisiacal ingredients I have nothing, I hasten to add; the only problem being that if the 'event' had taken place at either of these venerable spectacles I would have *been* the strawberries and cream; would have been lost in the sensation of my own sweetness and my lubriciousness as some be-hatted dame plopped me into her mouth – but then I would also simultaneously have been the dame and her big mouth too, no doubt. And hat.

'What happens?' I wanted to parrot Ronnie's earlier Anglo-Saxon response and say 'fuck-all' which (as I mentioned before) ironically fusing a positive and a negative, evokes it perfectly. But I have manners, so I simply replied:

'What happens? Nothing... everything,' The shrink smiled at my seemingly deliberate unhelpfulness.

I had been referred to the shrink by my GP and he - the shrink – and I had taken an immediate, irremediably polite dislike to each other. He didn't believe me, and I didn't care that he didn't believe me.

After a couple of sessions he ventures to suggest to me that I might be suffering from the clinical condition of 'DPD', or 'Depersonalisation Disorder', as if this official, albeit controversial, recognised nomenclature solved everything.

Although the condition was originally registered back in the 19<sup>th</sup> century, apparently, the most celebrated modern example of it was provided by an American writer, by the name of Suzanne Segal, in the 1980s and 90s. One day, upon a bus ironically, she had started having violent out-of-the-body experiences; well, not totally out-of-the-body; more partially removed, sort of two-feet-beside-herself, so that she witnessed everything she did, saw or felt from just behind herself, so to speak. This was unnerving to say the least.

A highly creative individual, Ms Segal proceeded to explore, both through literature and counselling, the landscape of her 'condition', which came and went over the years. Ultimately, her examination of her sense of 'self' was terminated when she was diagnosed many years later with a brain tumour, from which she eventually died.

Fascinating as Ms Segal's case was to me, it bore vital differences from my own experience. Indeed, I tried to convince the shrink that I suffered no such partial fracture in my experience of my 'self'; and that my dissociation was blissfully complete during the event; was, in fact, not a dissociation at all, since I - whatever 'I' was - felt both quietly and ecstatically identified with everything.... Indeed, I *was* the spirit of *association* – not dissociation.

This did not go down well with the shrink. No, the implicit thrust of his narrative was that I was ill and must, for my own good, of course, be eventually made to confess it, so that I could get better.

Shrinks are thus like mild-mannered, quietly spoken members of a modern inquisition whose job it is to restore you to the ranks of believers in our vast secular religion of normality; normality which is, perhaps, in addition to being a universal faith, also an open hospital for the terminally orthodox and well-adapted. I, however, not believing I was ill, only proved my own state of pathological denial.

One day, towards the end of our sessions, I turned the tables on him.

'What do *you* believe in, Mike?'

'Me?

'Yes, what gets you out of bed in the morning?'

'Well, that's an interesting question, Matt. The short answer is you, of course. I'm here to help you - and others like you. But then I'm not the one paying for the consultation here, and I think we'd better not waste our time on me; it's you I want to get to know....'

'Really?' My thought bubbles popped out above my head: 'Just how deeply *do* you want to get to know me, doctor, because I have a hunch this thing goes pretty deep?'

I looked hard at him and he returned my gaze with one of those clinically substantiated, letters-after-his-name smiles that says 'I know who's going to win this staring match, Matt, and it'll be me....'

He was right. I looked away first. I always look away first: it seems only polite.

Perhaps that's it: I'm just pathologically polite. Maybe politeness is a cancer that has invaded me body and mind. I suffer from secondary and tertiary diplomacy that has weakened every bone in my body and eaten away my moral muscularity.

I stopped going after a few weeks. It seemed fruitless. More importantly, it bored me. The rational approach to the event was so much less impressive and empowering than the event itself – which, actually, though I wanted to set in some sort of deeper context, I didn't merely want explained away.

So, no, I didn't conveniently own up to DPD; as I say, I didn't feel I had been de-personalised by the event in Auckland Avenue. I felt... I felt as if new life had taken root in me. Accordingly, predictably perhaps, my dreams were... not disturbing, no, it was my dream-life itself: the longer I stayed on at the bank the more turbulently active it became. Each night I was swept away on a river of images, sensations and feelings I could not control. Not that these dreams were always, or even often, interesting, or the people in them more than themselves, performing their pre-set mundane tasks. No, for the most part it was the intensity of the act of dreaming that mystified me – as if I had suddenly come into possession of an energy that had been placed at my disposal, an energy I could use – that, if I didn't, threatened to use me....

## 84 – A complete Balzac

*After the failure of Eno's 'Thursday Afternoon', I am still desperate to innovate my way out of my isolated bus-driver hell. I do not give up there... no.* Believing (with Balzac) that 'the eyes are the windows of the soul,' I decide to break and enter the ones belonging to my passengers. This I resolve to do by enacting another grave experiment upon the loveless living dead who daily mounted my platform. I will try – and this shows how desperate I had become – to connect with them! By which I mean radically maintain that common bond of warm-hearted humanity between well-meaning strangers who meet by chance – in this case on my bus! Those whose transactions with each other are of necessity so transient can still relate to each other, can't they? Is this too much to ask? Of course. But I am determined live out this fantasy of friendliness! How? By transgressing the taboo of looking into my passengers' eyes as they board my bus – and not just looking - but smiling.

This is insanity. Why on earth should you, the weary bus-pass toting traveller, be interested in me? Be honest: do you ever really look at me? I mean, when you get on board, when you show your pass or pay your money and get on my bus? Do you? No. Why would you?

Maybe vaguely, you register the sort of guy I am: fat, thin, small, big, ugly  - not handsome – bus drivers are never handsome (Donna is – to hell with sexist guilt! - the female exception that proves the generally masculine rule). But generally speaking you don't look me in the eye when you board the bus. As I say, why would you? It's a split second transaction, and I exist to facilitate it, to move you on, keep the logjam of people flowing through the city's streets towards their destinations. In the city's forest of destinations I am the lumberjack of stuck souls...

Which is why, when, conversely, I now look at you, you find it disconcerting. I mean, really look at you, look you in the eye when you come through my doors... and not only look – but smile. That's an unpardonable insult, the ultimate invasion of your privacy. Everyone knows you don't smile at strangers in the city. Privacy is paramount. In cities, privacy comes at a hard-won premium; privacy, which is the gold standard of vital anonymity, affording us protection from our urban, emotional bankruptcy.

Then a passenger hands me over a ten pound note (these are pre-Oyster days) for a short stop. I call in his promissory note by smiling at him – right in the eyes.

'What?' asks the bloke, expecting my driverly rebuke whilst picking up his change from my stainless-steel scoop next to my ticket machine.

173

'So how's it going?' I pursue my insane conversational track to its dead-end.

'Sorry?'

'Your day? How's it going?'

'Shitty. Since you ask, mate – or it will be if this bus doesn't get a fuckin' move on...'

And so he's gone: one nil to urban alienation. I try again, with the woman behind him. Unfortunately, she's very attractive and automatically thinks I'm hitting on her: no woman wants to be picked up by a bus-driver in any way over and above the function suggested by a bus-stop.

'How are you today madam?'

'I'm fine, thanks.'

'Good day ahead?'

'All right.' She looks queerly at me – but then I am behaving queerly – that is to say, humanly, as she flashes a pass, but no smile at me.

'Well, weekend coming up, doing anything nice?'

'Maybe. Look driver, do you mind, I need to get a seat.'

'Yes, yes, of course – apologies.' She negotiates the central aisle and settles in a seat next to the bloke I spoke to previously. In my mirror I see them exchange a brief look of ironic incredulity at their mad driver. Urban Alienation 2 - Over-Friendly Drivers United 0.

And that is today's human football results.

I try a few more times to open good relations with the passengers who clamber on board. Interestingly, the old are more open to suggestion: does this willingness derive from the loneliness that comes with their terrain, or are they perhaps members of the last generation that really valued social as well as sexual intercourse? The past being irrecoverable, we shall never know. What I do know is that the vast majority of my passengers just want it to be over. The bus journey and the day, I mean. And while it's not, they want privacy to bear it on their own terms as much as possible - privacy that provides us with the passport to travel swiftly without let or hindrance through our day towards the accomplishment of our aims. Who needs a bus driver to get in the way of that?

That said, what is it about something as simple as a smile that could interfere with that? Is our sense of privacy so fragile that the tenderness of a smile can shatter it? Tenderness – is that it? However much we arm ourselves, we remain vulnerable to tenderness – and we know it. But it's not just that. Tenderness is the preserve of intimates: anyone who presumes to show us tenderness, to purvey intimacy in inappropriate circumstances must be either mad or bad....

Yes, I now understand why smiling is bad for you in cities. It renders you vulnerable to retaliation. Far better to keep your capacity to love in reserve for those who don't expect its ambush – your hapless family or lovers. Love is thus a slaughter of the innocents.

∞

## 85 – Infidelity

Kate was understandably troubled by my cessation of sessions with the shrink; my insistence that my state of mind was not down to mental instability of any kind. Not that she thought I was mad; just that she didn't think I was sane either; and that, until I discovered how to make the limbo in between work for us both, she would take time out. So she came down one morning with a suitcase – and a baby son – our baby son.

'Matt, I'm going for a while.'

Surveying all the obvious clues with an expression of bovine curiosity, I looked up at Kate:

'What do you mean "going"?'

'To France. To Annette's for a couple of weeks. It'll give me a rest. From you. When I get back we have to sort this out – once and for all…'

'You don't have to go….' I remonstrated without even a hundredth part of conviction – 'unless you want to.'

Kate just looked at me, then a knock at the door confirmed her intentions. 'That's the taxi.... I'll speak to you later.'

And with that she picked Tom up.

'Can you help me with these bags?'

As I escorted her down the hall Tom looked at me: he had no choice because the angle at which Kate carried him pointed him up at me like a small missile of reproach. And yet his eyes packed no such charge. Instead, he just regarded me growing more distant with every step – almost like an initial, infantile exercise in regret: that all-too-human emotion we practise all our lives until we become perfect at it.

So Kate closed the door, and as silence surged back into the flat I discerned the slow warm rhythm of a horse breathing.

## 86 – Repo-man

With Kate temporarily gone, I had no excuse; with the flat empty of any distraction; with no crying baby to disturb my peace of mind, I suddenly had all the space and time I needed to mend myself, to reconcile the different parts of me; yes, now there was all the time in the world for Humpty to put himself back together again.

So I watched television. Or was it the television who watched me? We have an old relationship that goes back a long way, the TV and me. so that sometimes it's hard to know who's thinking what, we're so alike.

I didn't just watch television of course; I did other things, like surf the net. I Googled Hitler's rise to power many times – those Nazis, eh? where would our distracted, morbid outrage be without them! - I also investigated all the actors that had been screen tested unsuccessfully for James Bond and 'Wiki'd' the causes of The Renaissance until I was Cerulean blue in the face.

Then a bloke knocked at the door.

'Mr Matt Grant?' I had no clever play-script answer to this, so owned up to my role in his cheap mini-drama.

'I'm here as a representative of Makins. We are in turn representatives of First loans.' The penny drops.

"May I come in? It'll only take a minute...'

Actually, it takes about 15. Fifteen excruciating revolutions of the clock hands to listen to this vaguely threatening buffoon tell me I have now officially embarked on a reduced repayment scheme for six months while I get my finances in order, and that if I do not adhere to it, 'a court order will be obtained to secure the right to seize your car and/or chattels equal in value to said car...'

I let the buffoon out and scurry back on-line to scrutinise our bank balance. Sure enough we will only just make our next mortgage payment.

Money worries cut to the core of who we are. And by now I am nearly nobody. I must get a job. Any job. But I cannot – will not – go back to The City, even if they'd have me. So with Kate away, I start to scour the jobs pages and apply for anything that moves. And I mean anything.

Kate eventually returns from France to find me working first as a lolly-pop lady, then – my watch having been abolished in favour of traffic lights – as a packer of soft-porn magazines at a suburban distribution depot. The suburbs rely on porn – it's the only thing that keeps them alive.

After my work as a link in the sex industry dried up (the distribution centre removed to lower ground), I was a porter, a scooter pizza deliverer, caretaker, car-washer and candle-stick maker - and last and decidedly least: a bog cleaner. The tenacity of shit on porcelain: now that's a fitting metaphor for the soul tainted by imperfection!

What is about men and toilets? Why can they – we – not pay our visit to this Holy Land without the need for desecration? I'm not talking about graffiti: who cares about that bumpkin doodling of the third-rate urban mind? I mean the sanctity of the water closet's cleanliness. I'm no prude, but is there anything redemptive about the toilet experience to ward off our despair? If human nature seeks nobility, then the toilet is our tragedy: man's lowest ebb and katabasis lies in the bowl and pipes we all piss and shit on, and in, and through, down there.

Ah the cleaning of loos! The mess of other men's lives; the deduction of foul play from the stench of circumambient clues. Yes, I was a detective at many a crime scene, when something other than blood was spattered all over the walls. Mop, spray and cloth, my instruments of forensic intent! After a while, in one particular department, no malefactor was safe from my sleuthing. I could trace certain defecatory after-smells in the loo to particular bottoms. It was when I suddenly realised I was congratulating myself for this accomplishment that I knew all was lost.

There is only so much virtue in being dogged. After a certain point, you become a dog, get used to being kicked around by fate, happy if fate even bothers to kick you at all.... But occasionally, kennelled in a cage of your own worthlessness, you can't help but look up to the stars and howl for a way out. That's when you see the advert in the queue in front of you, driving home one, cold rainy night from finishing the last shitty row of loos...

'Looking for a new career? - Earn £500 a week, with overtime, driving a London bus..' And, as you know, I thought - why not? How hard can it be..?

Fool.

*Part 2 --- Hell Ride*

### 87 – Curing illness by ignoring it

*And so, of course, my bowel illness begins to take its course. This kind of nervous complaint can do for you in this business.* No-one admits to nerves at the depot. You're ill? Sure, take time off. But that quickly means half-pay, then investigation, possible redundancy, and with an exhausted wife at home and a six month old baby son to support, that's not an option.

Of course, I didn't need a consultant to diagnose the cause: simple nerves. Nerve endings; nervousness, nervous response – nerves are important; nerves are what make you human; they are your first line of defence against the onslaught that life mounts on us; as such, we employ them daily in our linguistic legions; nerves articulate our response to the attack; they respond to the nerve gas which infects our states of mind: 'You get on my nerves'; 'it plays on my nerves'; 'my nerves are shot'; 'nervous exhaustion'; 'nerveless'; 'nerve-centre'; 'nervous laughter'; 'nerve-racking'; 'nervous impulse'; 'nervous system'; nervous breakdown'; - nerves....

Yes, my nerves are shot. The bomb scare doesn't help.

### 88 – The strange banality of other people's emergencies

*The day starts badly. Emergencies always happen when it's most inconvenient.* That is the nature of an emergency: if it were planned in advance it wouldn't be an emergency.

182

Take this old man's heart attack on my bus. One moment he's paying me in spare coppers for a ride, the next, I'm giving him artificial resuscitation. He's just collapsed getting on my bus. Legs buckle under him and his face goes red then blue as old ladies put their hands to their face and young blokes pull off their headphones in the first digital stages of alarm.

The sensation of his old man's stubble is really all I feel of my chance kiss-of-life with this old buffer. I inflate his lungs like a father blowing up a lilo for his little son. The ambulance is on its way forever, never quite arriving – or so it seems. He doesn't come round, at least not on the bus.

The paramedics eventually arrive and cart him off. I will never hear of him again: whether he will live or die I know not. He certainly never rings to thank me for my intervention. I don't blame him. For all I know, my resuscitation was too artificial and that was what did for him. At least I did my best. Not to kill him, I mean. Unfortunately, this kind of mindless adaptability translates as coolness under fire. I hear a woman passenger's voice generously but unnecessarily extolling me.

'Did you see the bus-driver? He was a wonderful! I wouldn't've liked to give that old boy mouth-to-mouth!'

Nor did I, as it happens. But I had no choice. No-one else would do it, and it was my bus. The threatened charge of cowardice is a powerful motivation and requires no little courage to resist it... fortunately I *was* a coward and sprang into action.

## 89 - Bomb Scare

*In a daze I drive on. You can't turn back the bus for an incident like this.* Already late, people are dependent on you: desks throughout The City wait to be filled by workers who will open cases, close files, veto and seal deals - this needs to happen on time. Thus, tube and bus drivers are custodians of priceless punctuality. No, you drive on.

So it's not good when the bus inspector heaves into view unexpectedly.

The look on her face, the way she knocks urgently on the window - I know I'm in trouble: driver protocol is sacred: bus inspectors don't depart from it unless they mean business. I press the button: the hydraulic doors open with that sharp, spiteful release of air that still shocks me every time I hear it - even though I'm ready for it. Urgently, she beckons me to come down from my cabin. I've done nothing wrong, but it's in my guilty nature to expect – almost welcome - a reprimand. Have I run someone over without realising it, casually killed the whole queue of old bats lined up outside early-morning Bingo, 'en passant', as it were? I scan her face for signs....

'The whole of the West End is in lock-down...' she informs me, instantly reverting to her mobile whilst signalling me to interrupt her conversation at my – and the world's – peril.

'OK... OK... will do. So whether it's bombs gone off or just bomb scares, we don't know?'

Whatever they look like, all inspectors come dressed in a uniformed self-importance that goes with giving orders: this one barely registers me. These are the years in the aftermath of 7/7's atrocities and this is her moment. She's the vital link in the chain of command: all that stands between London, democracy and chaos. As for me: I am merely lowly driver number 314 in charge of the 8.45 am. 257 to Oxford Circus, here to await her command. Finally, she gives it triumphantly.

'There will be no roads open to or from any of the major bridges until further notice.... You'll have to terminate!'

Terminate? I look at her with a default expression of profound stupidity. Where am I s'posed to go? – And I do need to go! Right now I need to shit for England. With a pre-planned toilet stop just yards away, my bowels are in silent agony.

'Are you listening to me, driver?'

No.... I don't think so...let me check: no, I'm definitely not listening to her, because any moment now the bottom is going to drop out of my world – literally.

No, the bottom line is this: at bottom (typically, the word suddenly takes on an almost mystical versatility!) human nature is ruthless: hard-wired for self-preservation – and if humiliation represents a kind of extinction of selfhood, then the fast approaching diarrhoea means I'm in big trouble. This is about the annihilation of self-respect, about me losing every last vestige of humanity in front of all these nameless city faces, these rows of total strangers whose good opinion of me I suddenly value beyond all price. I have to go and I have to go now!

Besides! What else can I do? I don't know what the situation is further down the line; one of many false alarms each month, probably – but the truth is, sat here in this big, red hearse, I'm a dead man, psychologically-speaking - unless I can somehow undertake the decent despatch of my own crisis first. And right now I do not possess an undertaker's disinterested, professional detachment. Au contraire! My body is in a state of grief. This instant it's all I can do to keep the tragedy of my bowels in check. Every nerve, every sinew, every vein straining not to let the inevitable happen, not to relax my grip on the gathering tribulation below my waist.

'Make sure you tell the passengers calmly: don't go into details,' demands the inspector. 'And don't say 'terrorist attack! We don't know anything yet; probably another false alarm.... Passengers who want to stay on board to get back home can do so – free, of course...'

I stare back blankly at this grotesque display of ludicrous, mock generosity.

'Driver - you've got to tell the passengers!'

'The sports centre!' I suddenly hear myself reply to the inspector – or rather at her, because I couldn't give a shit (no pun intended) what she thinks of my new emergency route.

If I can only get this big red bastard of a double-decker bus to the sports centre! The Promised Land of toilet heaven! My bowels ache for the privacy of this suburban temple with its rows of sacred compartments: private, Formica confessionals of defecatory intimacy wherein my body will be shriven of its faecal sins!

The inspector disappears back into her mobile. Back on board the bus I turn on the PA microphone and get ready to address the passengers. But everything's out of sync – I'm out of sync. I find myself distractedly delivering the wrong message down the PA to the passengers:

'The sports centre,' I cracklingly murmur to them, 'I'll park up there - do it there!'

### 90 – Goldfish faces

*Almost invisibly, the inspector recedes back down the street into a fug of her own self-importance.* Distracted, in my cack-handed getaway, I delay another more lucid address to the passengers for a moment. Ten minutes 'max' to the sports centre – all being well. - 'All being well?!' Suddenly, I see I have turned on the windscreen wipers on this starkly sunny day. Quickly extinguishing this betrayal of panic, I scrabble them off again and search the world in front of me. The glass offers no hiding-place.

As I prepare to convey my PA message I make the fatal mistake of looking in my rear view mirror: they're all staring at me. Suddenly I dislike them intensely. These passengers I'm carrying. Passengers in life! My life! Fuck their A to B existences! What about me? What do they care? Staring with their gormless, expressionless faces; floating helplessly in the element of chance circumstance like goldfish gawping behind the bus's windows - and we all know where goldfish end up.... Then suddenly the goldfish in my current bowl revolt.

'Driver – what's happening?' demands a not-so-Koi carp half way down the bus.

He's right. This is the 21$^{st}$ century and goldfish – however small their bowls – have rights. So I clear my throat and burble perfect fish-language to the passengers.

'Ladies and gentlemen I can confirm there has been an incident in London and that just as a precaution we are terminating and returning, via stops along South Bank, Battersea Park and others. Please remain seated. I'll let you off when and where you want...'

A brief pause ensues then ---

'Fookin' bastard!'

188

First time I hear it I think I'm imagining it - but there it is again.

'I said you're a fookin' bastard!'

I peer in my rear-view mirror to see where this Yorkshire-shaped oath is coming from. Sure enough, from amongst the undergrowth of passengers, at the back of the bus comes the call of the rare 'fookin' bastard' swearing bird: a prize species sometimes glimpsed in moments of great stress, swearing at no-one in particular to mark out his territory.... Yes, we've got a nutter on board. That'll calm the passengers down in their moment of need.

'You total fookin' bastard!'

In my capacity as human bird-watcher I should've recognised him when he got on: he displayed that vital giveaway plumage, three plastic bags packed full to the bulging gunnels with bugger all except other plastic bags. Now it's too late. My bowels are bursting, I've got a bomb scare and a fruitcake on board.

Meanwhile my stomach is in steady turmoil. I'm desperate, sweating. Get a grip. Get a hold of yourself, Or this is could go badly wrong. It is going badly wrong.

Suddenly, I have to brake next to a movie billboard out of which a great white shark stares into the bus, communicating news of the latest man-eater to arrive in the violent, cinematic waters of bored popular consciousness. As if in sympathy, a razor sharp pain shoots up from the depths of my false calm. Not that you see it. No, my controlled anxiety is like the cool, placid ocean surface that hides the monster of panic, half-visible in the nightmarish gloom beneath you....

## 91 - The option of no option

*No. I cannot just stop the bus. Think about it: my passengers have just heard about an incident in London;* through texts, phone calls and radios they're hearing all sorts of rumours about bomb-scares in the West End - and here is their bus driver suddenly stopping in the high street and leaping out of his cab, abandoning the bus and them, they know not why. – So they jump to the obvious conclusion: they too are about to become victims of some fanatic. Panic ensues, the high street erupts, anger explodes, cars crash into each other as they attempt to manoeuvre; people are crushed in their attempt to escape the chaos. No. I cannot just stop the bus....

## 92 – No room to fart

*Then a voice shouts from the back of the bus:*

'Oy! Driver! – Can we stop 'ere, please, you're going in the opposite direction to where I want to go!' – Said man rises from his seat but is barged into by an irate old dear also wanting to get off. I jam on the brakes too suddenly, inducing a cruelly comic moment in the tradition of undiluted farce.

Staggered by the g-force of my sudden stop, and travelling slightly downhill past Battersea Dogs' Home as we are, the woman, proudly and plumply past her prime, slips and plonks down onto her ample behind, upon which she then slides down the aisle and is deposited baggage-like beside my cabin.

As I look down I want to ask 'Can I help you Madam?' in the aristocratic, languidly indifferent tones of an Oscar Wilde character - but none of them drove buses. So I look democratically concerned instead. Behind her the bloke, aggressive with anxiety, helps her up. She looks at me with a mixture of scorn and injured pride.

'You ought to be ashamed, driver!'

'I'm very sorry Madam, I'm dealing with a difficult situation here, as I'm sure you can see.'

'Yes, and not dealing with it very well neither!' she accurately retorts as both of them descend from the bus. I close the hydraulic doors on their contempt.

I'm now desperate at least to fart! If I could fart that might release a little of the pressure in my bowels. O Jesus, I have farted! Not just farted either: enough's come out to remind me of another aspect of childhood. No, not remind me: project me rocket-style back into the great stratospheric diarrhoeas of the past. Being sent home by Mrs Beaumont, my overbearing, goldfish-bowl-bespectacled, primary school teacher, whose small dun-coloured eyes twinkled like pinpoints of piranha spite as she bade me leave the classroom with my soiled underpants in a brown paper bag! - Please no. Not that. Not now. Underpants can only take so much stress, and this is their limit before they betray me. Your bus-driver cannot smell of shit. No sir. That's not part of the deal. Not even on a day like this.

I breathe in and tense every muscle below my chest. Hold it! Hold it…. Turn left past Battersea Dogs Home – I swear I can hear them barking encouragement at me as I drive by! Everyone loves a tryer!

Only a few minutes to go…. Breathe deeply! The dam holds. But then disaster.

Bright orange 'high-visibility' exclusion tapes criss-cross the road I want to take – 'police incident!' Another on the bomb-scare list… - I cannot get directly – or indirectly - to the Sports Centre; cannot proceed straight to go. With a jolt, again I bring the bus to a sudden halt. What the fuck am I going to do now?

### 93 – No through road

*Standstill. Silent panic. My route to the sports centre blocked, I sit paralysed by indecision. The bus engine ticks over with sinister indifference.*

"Now what? Why have you stopped here?" asks an disgruntled passenger.

'For fuck's sake - some of us want to get home!'

'Fookin' bastard!' chirps the swear-bird.

I turn round with a glare: any moment now I may just get out of my cab and shit right there and then, in front of the bastards. It is now darkly clear to me that I must drive on to my next nightmare alternative toilet, the aptly named 'World's End' pub, which lies adjacent to a long, large bus stop that I can park up in, about a mile away just before Clapham Common.

(Inexplicably, perhaps as a reaction to my desperation, I suddenly chortle at our Tourette's sufferer, and it suddenly occurs to me to wonder if Tourette's itself is not really a form of social conscience in which the sufferer speaks his mind on behalf of all of us....)

## 94 – The sound of another child crying

*Ten minutes or so 'til the World's End pub. I'm holding the steering wheel so hard the veins upon my wrists begin visibly to pulse and throb.* Puncturing the ring of my protective silence I hear the sound of a child crying, which is the worst sound in the world as far as I'm concerned – and not always for the usual charitable reasons.

What's this? A woman, a young mum, is sidling up the aisle to me. Her child, an ill-favoured pug-faced boy of about five, stifles his tears. His mother informs me discretely, the boy wants to go to the toilet (don't we

193

all!), but not soon, not in the next quarter of an hour, say; no, right now; this instant. In fact, the child is about to shit unless I can stop and find a public loo. (Ah, a young man after my own heart!)

'I'll let you off as soon as I can, madam, I promise,'

They temporarily occupy the elderly and disabled seats, nudging a large old lady with many bags thereon. She is not impressed. The mum and dung-boy, not noticing her irritation, are forlorn of mien – a timeless, antique emotion reserved for special occasions such as this. The boy starts to cry again. The other passengers tacitly approve their forlorn-ness and Victorianly pretend their tension isn't mounting.

Traffic lights....

'Driver, perhaps you'd better just let us out here!' pleas diarrhoea boy's mum with understandable desperation. But I can't just let them get out here at the lights; there's a slip road to my left and traffic is sluicing through it: if I eject them they'll be dead in a second.

'Any minute now, madam, I promise you.' I reassure her impotently. If she only knew how close she was to being surrounded by diarrhoeic assailants, to being shat on from two fronts! Breathe... breathe.... Where is this pain? Let's focus on it; shift it out of my consciousness the way the manuals say. Buy myself a few more minutes with the mystery of concentration.

Where is it? Let me block it! My guts! No, lower down than that: it's that area between your stomach and your arsehole – is it the rectum? Yes, the rectum! Dark passageway leading to the traitor's gate of the anus! The corridor down which all enemies of the Crown must pass to their rightful doom! The river-sewer of the soul! My rectum is aching for release! But I cannot raise the portcullis of my anus yet! I cannot eject the traitorous turds to their rightful resting-place! The world's End pub – get me to The World's End....

### 95 - Boa constrictor in Clapham

*At last! Green! 'Go! Go! Go!' - as F1 commentator Murray Walker advised Michael Schumacher, starting from another grid!* But only seconds later my accelerating bus gets swallowed up by a monster of a queue that blocks my way down Kennington High Street! A great boa constrictor bulging with the distended intentions of ten thousand souls! The street's peristalsis has ceased to function. Its digestive system is clogged with the delayed food of human purpose. - Unlike mine.

With my bowels and those of my fellow diarrhoea sufferer at breaking-point, I take an executive decision and do what, for obvious reasons, no bus-driver is supposed to do in a high street: I back up! Yes, yes, yes I'm sorry! I'm sorry! I raise an apologetic arm to alarmed drivers, but I have to get out of this serpentine queue before I am constricted to death, and the fact is for once I don't have to keep to the bus's normal beaten track! I can take whichever-the-hell route I want to get to the

World's End pub. By backing up I can take the slip road I just passed.

## 96 - Blitz spirit

*'Madam, I can't talk at the moment I'm afraid...'*

Unbelievable! - in addition to our crying child and resident foul-mouthed nutter, a row has now broken out over the disabled seats. In times of stress the puritan sense of protocol rises to the surface. In wars, the warden mentality prevails.

'I'm sorry driver, but it's not right; these seats are reserved for the elderly or infirm!' says the old bat with the turquoise mac and blue hair. She and her shopping are spread over two and a half seats next to said mum and crying boy.

But why turquoise? Why does a certain type of elderly woman immediately throw on the turquoise mac and blue-rinse the moment she hits seventy? Is it part of a birthday disguise kit they all get sent by Her Majesty the Queen?

'Bear with us, madam, I think you'll find the lady's getting off very shortly,' I plea very reasonably.

But the mother can't resist a dig at her old assailant's ample girth.

'God, how many seats do you need?'

'I beg your pardon! Look, it's women like you that can't control their kids...' society breaking down, country gone to the dogs, et cetera, et cetera.

I leave them to it, hoping it'll die down, but a sense of hysteria is building in the bus. Predictably it's all too much for our foul-mouthed favourite from the Dales.

'Fookin bastards!' he screams from the back of the bus.

### 97 – Critical mass

*And then it all kicks off.*

Heretofore lost in the winding coils of my alimentary canal; consumed, as it were, in the private purgatory of my dysfunctional bowel, I have forgotten my passengers completely. Fortunately the Fookin Bastard bird reminds me.

'Fookin' coont!' he chirps up extemporaneously.

'I beg your pardon!' admonishes our fat, turquoise bat (this ludicrous anachronistic understatement eludes her). 'I've never heard anything so disgusting in my life! Driver! Driver!'

Sure enough, her anger sets off crying pug-faced boy again.

'Can't you stop that boy crying?' she demands rhetorically.

'No, I bloody can't – you'd be crying too if you were desperate for the toilet! Driver we need to get off – anywhere!' pleas mum.

'Fookin' bastard!' from the back.

'Driver, please eject that foul-mouthed man!'

Then a shocking apology which, I can feel in the air, momentarily disarms us all.

'I'm sorry – Tourette's – I can't help it,' blurts out the Fookin-Bastard bird, bookending his revelation with a slightly amended obscenity.

'Fookin bitch! …Sorry…. - Coont!'

Turquoise bat-woman is momentarily and proverbially stunned into silence.

### 98 – The gods themselves aghast…

*'Fookin-bitch-coont!' squawks our Yorkshire Dales bird of paradise in the general direction of the disabled seats.*

Fat, turquoise bat rightly assumes the insult is for her.

'Driver, stop this bus!'

198

'I've got fookin' Tourette's - fookin'bitch!'

'I don't care what you've got, you're a foul-mouthed yob. Driver!'

In a fusion of anger and blind panic I slam on the brakes. I feel the gods themselves, as if in shock, draw back aghast. This could be fatal – but isn't. There is no pile-up behind me: a horn honks, but that is all.

In a slow march of grave intent all the warring passengers then dismount the bus: fat, turquoise bat, upset mum and dung-boy and the fookin-bastard bird.

I watch them evaporate into the pavement crowd like cantankerous spirits exorcised from my bus. But other ghouls remain....

### 99 - Sphincter-tight roads

*I'm now driving slightly too fast, which, in a car, wouldn't mean much – but in a bus...* - In a bus, four or five miles over the limit dictated by the circumstances can result in a dead child.

I slow down. As a result my pulse speeds up a bit more. My sphincter is in overdrive; my rectum on overload, my anus's firm grip on proceedings shows signs of loosening. – St Hilary's Road: I am about five minutes from the World's End. I can do this. I WILL do this...

## 100 – Defeated

*Crisis! The end of the road! The sign at the edge of the world, over which my hope plunges, reads 'The World's End pub is closed for refurbishment until August';* thus leaving me with a putative three weeks 'til my next shit... This is pushing it. I am, in fact, a dead man. Finally, it's clear to me I have no further refuge; that there is nowhere else to go, no way out.

I am defeated. Vanquished. Crushed. I carry on driving down the road stunned. Like a refugee being strafed by the Stuka of ill-chance, I disburden all my hopes along the way. Though moving, I stand mentally abandoned. I know there is no chance of reaching safety, of getting to the neutral zone of any public WC. I am lost. I must surrender, full of shit. In a moment I must raise my hands and let go of all of it....

Ahead lies only the suburban badlands of Clapham Common. The respectable, Victorian-fronted, toilet-less perdition of despair.... And as I drive on, my sunken hearts sinks deeper, knowing my diarrhoeic soul will find no redemption there...

I am now driving blindly through the neatly-tailored wilderness of Clapham Common. I am about to shit. All refuges denied to me, I am about to lose my grip on a whole pile of it. - How I hate London's parks; their pastiche of nature girdled by tame streets!

It's coming. The dam is breaking. The bottom is about to drop out of my world.... I must stop the bus.

Now.

### 101 – Point of no return

*This is it. My arse is at the point of no return. My arse IS the point of no return... I stop the bus in the bus lane skirting Clapham Common.*

'What's 'e doin' now?' I hear some 'Cheerful Charlie' ask in mock disbelief towards the back of the bus.

What indeed?

I undo the driver's cabin half-door and grab the bag of last resort. Turning to face my passengers I think of what to say, but no words come. I mumble 'be a minute...' and then open the pneumatic doors....

'Pssshit!' say the air-pressured doors, laughing their usual prophecy at me as I bound out of the cabin much to the amazement of my charges....

### 102 – Rear-guard action

*I have dismounted from my cabin and I am running. At least I think I am, I seem to make so little progress -* running across grass – away from my bus. I turn and see the obstructed traffic try to get past my beached, abandoned Behemoth: I couldn't park it any closer to the curb – one wheel is on the curb. The passengers peer out at my fleeing form through the dirty window-glass. They see a uniformed bus-driver careering crazily towards a tree – the sole tree on that part of Clapham Common, an oasis of refuge in a green, suburban desert of un-tranquillity. It's here that I must pitch my camp beneath no stars! – Bedouin carrying nothing but one bagful of Boots toiletries! Here, I must stake my claim to peace of mind - and evacuate the rest!

### 103 – One Tree Common

*So this is it! This is the tree that life has led me to. The tree of life whose fruit of the knowledge of good and evil I am forced to eat, though it cause my expulsion from my own personal garden of Eden!* But Clapham Common is not the garden of any Eden I would be that sad to leave – especially once I'd shat in it. And that I am about to do – am forced to do.

I peer furtively about me – though just how furtive one can be in plain view of a bus-full of commuters on one hand and a park-full of playground mums, children and general joggers on the other is a mystery.

The tree itself - is it a Lime or Plane or Ash? Why do I care? – offers no refuge from exposure, no hiding place from the sun-racked glare of public scrutiny. The tree is too thin, too young – little more than a sapling of ten years maybe, it hardly hides my body on any side. Too late to care, I take my bag of last resort - and drag the paper out.

## 104 – Humiliation

*All eyes are on me. I feel their disbelief. My 'high-vis' yellow jacket marks me out for degradation by the crowd – exacerbated, as I pull my trousers down, by the beacon of my bare bum.* My answer is to hunch, make myself small. But however small I try to be I remain a giant of my own absurdity. Stay calm! Go to your quiet place. There is no quiet place.

So I bend the knees,

squat down,

and take aim....

## 105 – Bomb-aimer

*To squat is to become less than human. Squatting is inherently indelicate; that said, it is also full of the power of grievous intent.* In peering down at the intimate cartography between my knees I am become a bomb-aimer over war-time Hamburg, London and Berlin. I have only a moment to release my projectiles and get out of here. Meanwhile, the searchlight-gaze of my passengers and a myriad passers-by shines on my sinister intent, about to shoot me down. I am about to die - metaphorically.... No, in a way – actually: insofar as I possess a social identity - I am about to die – again.

### 106 – The cross-hairs of incredulity

*Pensioners, mothers, athletes training, lovers lying on the grass, children laughing, playing tag – all stop: I am in their sights, the cross-hairs of their incredulity.* The moment is electric with their and my disbelief. Am I really doing what I/they think I'm doing? Mounting a full-on attack on the citadel of bourgeois propriety? Am I about to shit in public in broad daylight? Time freezes. I press the button. The bomb doors of my anus open....

### 107 – Nothing evil this way comes....

*Time stands still. Like one of those movie moments when suddenly all the people in a street stop in mid-flow and turn to look at you.*

I am the focus of their gaze: life is, indeed, my movie and they are taking part in it. Their faces say it all as I squat down: is he...? Yes, is he...?

Yes, I am really going to shit. My arsehole is open to the four winds, So why is nothing coming out of it?

### 108 - The anus of Janus

*Crouched here behind the tree, I squat between two worlds.* Over one presides the god of sunlit self-respect, the power of purpose, meaning and forward motion; over the other lours an evil spirit of impotent regret and self-contempt, the fraught urge to retreat. This is echoed in my body: a frigid fusion of terror and bravado, it does not know which way to go; my colon and rectum push for release; but still my bourgeois conscience signals 'no'!

The anal wind in my infantile, Freudian willows whistles....

I look back at my passengers on the bus; they return my gaze: are they aware, I think, that time is a great comedian, his joke on all of us?

## 109 – Bombs away!

*Suddenly it comes and the dichotomy is over; suddenly it comes and my bottom is in clover - actually and metaphorically, my faecal crisis over!*

Shit pores out of my arse onto the grass beneath me. It is only semi-diarrhoea, so its trajectory is an acceptable fusion of the linear and radial – in a neat '99' ice-cream whirl around and up to but not upon my feet. I am almost proud of this act of containment, this faecal victory when all around predicted my defeat. Then I look up and look around – I had forgotten the world had stopped and thus suddenly see that still it hasn't started on its axis once again. The searchlights of innumerable eyes are fixed on me. Time to take emergency evasive action!

## 110 – One of our bombers is missing

*Before I can vacate my dumping ground there is the small question of hygiene to consider.* My last vestige of dignity demands that I cannot get back on board my bus with any trace of excrement upon my hands or smell about my person. From my bag of last resort I draw the alcohol cleanser and squirt solution all over my hands and wrists. I check my shoes and trousers and my fluorescent 'high-vis' bomber jacket. All is clear. The loo paper I have used is placed inside a plastic bag for later disposal. I can now get out of here. I rev up my engines for a swift departure....

### 111 – I'm a non-entity – get me out of here

*Taking one last furtive look around before take-off, I see that pensioners in particular seem revolted by my primeval dump;* their standards may relate to an earlier prelapsarian tradition, but not that prelapsarian...! The young mothers on the common, too, are only slightly less appalled; they pull their potty-trained Pollies and Peters anxiously towards them in disgust - and rightly so. Having mounted a daytime raid on the morals of an exclusively civilian area I, myself, am full of ambivalence at the mission I have accomplished. Sharply, I pull the Lancaster bomber of my bum around and bank swiftly, vertiginously into the sky above. But it's too late! More disgusted glances puncture me, my integrity is badly holed. I limp (a verb the old war movies taught us to use) back to the hangar of my bus where my passengers await like inoperational ground-crew too stunned to react to the catastrophe coming in to land....

## 112 – The power of the rear-view mirror

*I get back on board my bus with as much sangfroid as I can muster – which is none.* By this time my passengers' mouths are collectively open in united incredulity. Their day, originally diverted by the fear of another urban tragedy, is now concluded by my grotesque comic farce. So amazed are they that their bus driver has descended from his cab, run out onto the common and shat in plain view of all and sundry that they are deprived of speech.

Fleetingly, settling into my seat, I look in the rear-view mirror with a view to saying something to them, perhaps calmly explaining the necessity of what has just happened. Instantly, as if by magic, all their eyes, all their glances fuse with mine in that relatively tiny mirror, and it is plain that there is nothing to be said; nothing that can be said. It is what it is. Now and forever. I have entered their trivial scatological folklore on a grave day.

## 113 – A silence heralding a kind of holiness

*The rest of the journey back to the depot passes in a silence so profound it almost attains to a kind of holiness.* Amongst people who have shared certain sights there is nothing to be said…. Passengers get off the bus without saying thank you. This is as it must be in our shared atmosphere of exhausted embarrassment at what has passed: there is not enough metaphorical oxygen for dialogue.

Ahead I see the shadow of the depot at the end of a more than usually exhausting morning. Afternoon has already begun its disappearing act; soon evening will fall, the caravan of hours having travelled their course to reach that oasis-calm: evening, the shady temporal oasis where, without premeditation, a spirit of reflection magically descends and relaxes our destructive grip on time; evening, that period of timelessness itself, when, like Janus, you finally you possess the time to reflect simultaneously both ways in life, to look backwards and forwards at what you have done and will do....

### 114 – A-haunting we will go....

*My bus thus emptied at last of all passengers, I draw into the depot and park up as if nothing's happened –* which, of course, compared to what's really happened that day, is true.

It is eerily quiet as I dismount from my cabin and walk into the drivers' lounge, which exudes an air of desertion. In the light of the bomb scares in London only a skeleton staff has operated, most drivers having been sent home early. I put away my high-viz jacket which has more than done its job today. And pretend there's nothing wrong. And I take a profound discomfort in my own dissemblance. How long can it be before the passengers' complaints roll in? Do they even now await me in the form of a summary invitation to the manager's office..?

As yet, perhaps predictably, given the day's events, there's nothing. No notice-board message. No e-mail to see the manager. Nothing.... I slip out of the depot by a side-door, like a ghost through a wall. Another haunting has begun.

### 115 – A long walk home

*I didn't go straight home that day. I walked all the way back from the depot across London, from West to East, via as many of those self-same parks, in one of whose number I had found (no) refuge earlier that day.* I walked... and I thought – of whatever came into my head and heart.

For all the obvious reasons I felt a strange mixture of shame and elation. Obvious? What else could I have done on that common? No, having been driven by necessity, I felt exonerated from opprobrium, immune from shame – even proud – yes I admit it – proud at having... what? - survived the whole psychological catastrophe of excreting so publically.

Do I exaggerate? People will go a long way before they shit in public. Why? What is it about crapping that invests the act with such a sacred aura of prohibition for us in the West? Is it the noble fact of our uber-civilised humanity that's cast into such grave doubt by the bass reality of our shit? Are we, in shitting, forced to let go of every last shred of dignity in doing it? Are we, in shitting, revealed as less than all we hope, all we esteem ourselves to be? Do we, in the end, thus stand revealed in our own eyes as less than human? Is this shock too much for essentially spiritual beings too bear?

When I shat in public on Clapham Common, in a sense there was nowhere else to go. When people have seen you do that, seen you be reduced to an ape-like function, to an anal, simian grotesque, you can't pretend any more; can't pretend you have any esteem in their eyes, any sense of dignity or worth. And if you have no social esteem what value *do* you have? If everyone thinks you're a disgusting weirdo – well, then, *aren't* you a disgusting weirdo?

You know what the experts say – that personality is a social construct? That our souls are, in a sense, socialised into existence – certainly socialised into certain shapes according to the particular societal values we grow up with and are moulded by? Well, that only seems like part of the truth to me. Don't we contribute to who we are? Don't we input some of the socialisation rules ourselves? And if we do, whence *does* that confident personal sense of value and self-worth derive? It must come from somewhere deeper; must lie at a level far more profound than the social gaze of other men and woman can penetrate; somewhere so deep it doesn't depend on anyone else, doesn't even depend on you; somewhere called, perhaps, in my case, Auckland Avenue....

Ah Auckland Avenue! How did I travel so far away from you! So far that I ended up shitting in public on Clapham common? The comedy both of my thoughts and my predicament almost amuses me: I don't know whether to laugh or cry. So I do both. This is not a good sign.

And then, as the hours passed on my walk home a slow tide of psychological humiliation began to press upon me, a release of all the dumb, silent pressure I had – body and soul – been forced to absorb since driving the bus, culminating in my crap on Clapham common. Truly, I felt sorry for myself – profoundly, resonantly sorry. If it is right to exercise compassion for one's fellow human beings, is it not right to do the same towards oneself on occasion? Circumstance is a bitch-goddess. She had forced me to suffer profound indignity. Public ignominy. And so publically! A truism, I know, but cities are so superlatively public. Cities are where whatever happens to us is made public – eventually.

## 116 – Cities!

*That night, when I got home Kate had gone to bed. I slumped in front of the TV* and, hitherto consumed by my own trivially intense experience, saw what had really been going on in London that day. In that blurred, semi-drugged way that someone else's news insinuates itself on your anaesthetised consciousness, I slowly digested the details of the bomb scare and a couple of suspect bags safely blown up by bomb disposal units during my detour. Thankfully, there had been no terrorist attack – in London....

But in cities across the world it was predictably otherwise: I gawped televisually at another day's terror, another round of grief-stricken despair - my television told no lies. On that day, as on any day across the world, across our species' entire history, other cities had been under attack; children lay dead, men and women cried in the streets and walked around with their arms blown off.

So much misery is contemporaneous with our necessary indifference. Whilst we buy a coffee, drink a beer, make some tea or put out the cat, stray bullets snicker round the side-streets of Beirut and bereave parents of a beloved girl or boy; whilst we amble in antiques markets, corpses of the young are paraded in open coffins only a holiday flight away. And all our cities whisper the same history.

Cities! The matrix of human ambivalence: simultaneously so cruel and so kind; at once so populous and solitudinous, so intimate and indifferent, so primitively clumsy for strangers to negotiate and so easy for natives to exploit, yet still so ambivalent for both: gold mines of culture and backwaters of despair.

Cities! Where it all comes together – wherein we delight and decry; openly engineer or get away with on the sly; contribute to the cause of being human, or steal from human dignity. Cities! Both our refuge and our exile – none more so than London - aboriginal metropolis which, for millennia, foreigners have made their home, inter-marrying and mixing their genius with our own. London: city of mongrels! A trillion vying genes of human nature twist and turn in the spiral of your DNA!

212

Cities! mad, glad, sad bastions of the miraculous and unexceptional, of drabness, beauty and despair; let those of us who love you always protect you from the eternal philistine who thinks the only way to possess you is to destroy you!

Cities....

### 117 – Changeling

*I wasn't the same when I woke up.* Kate didn't know whether to proverbially laugh or cry about this latest devastating event in my otherwise banal existence.

'You look terrible,' she observed encouragingly.

'I feel terrible.'

'You need to get away.'

'What, from you?' I joked with spectacular bad timing.

'From yourself. – I'm going to make you!' Then, with an impulsiveness proportionate to my impotent exhaustion, Kate got on the phone and bollocked my consultant for further, quicker tests to sort out, kill or cure, my colonic troubles. Apparently, she then also made another call to book me a fortnight away – in Marrakesh. Perhaps she wanted a new carpet – or some hashish.

'I can't go to Marrakesh!'

'Why not?'

'It's in Morocco, for chrissake!'

'Two hours away. – I've booked it. This time tomorrow!'

'What about work?'

'Rung them already – you're on two weeks leave.'

'But we can't afford it – not even with the plastic.' I lamely objected.

'Matt – this is serious. We can't - *you* can't carry on like this. Unless you can change something...'

'I can change – I will change... I'm just... what about you and Tom?'

'Annette's coming over next week. I'll get her round. Don't argue or I'll change my mind!'

Then a pause.

'But don't come back unless you know why....'

'I *will* know why,' I replied with curiously childlike confidence to Kate's mysterious ultimatum.

Deception of those one loves is an interesting experience, it involves an emotional dissociation which is both thrilling and depressing – even if, in this case, my motives for lying to Kate were good. - Yes, I would go away, but unbeknownst to Kate, first I went round to the travel agent, exercised my statutory rights and cancelled Marrakesh, the romantic prospect of which, though affordable on credit, exceeded the means of my imagination. In truth, my distress was deeply unromantic. I knew that whatever change of scene, whatever period of leave I needed from the trenches of bus driving I could surely get much closer and more cheaply and, I intuited, no less productively, closer to home.

I didn't tell Kate. I was *going* to, but on returning home the momentary opportunity was eclipsed by her obvious delight at her own impulsive generosity. Add to this my exhaustion, and the result was that I suddenly found myself in possession of an absurdly meaningless secret. Of course, I would tell her later when I got back. She wouldn't mind: it would all work out... we would laugh about it! (wouldn't we?) Thus my preposterously trivial deception now assumed a life of its own. The hour of my departure comes round with indecent haste.

'Are you sure you won't let me take you to the airport?'

'No, no, seriously, I'm fine. I'll ring you when...when I get there....'

'There' being five miles down the road in Croydon.

How was I to know the joke, in time, would be on me?

*Part Three --- Down in the soul's basement*

Croydon is not as beautiful as Marrakesh - not by the longest of pastel-coloured Expressionist chalks. But why Croydon exactly? This, the most bourgeois of suburbs: this inoffensive South London of the soul! And a basement B & B in Croydon at that! Why? Because Croydon is where you end up when you have absolutely nowhere else to go, and is thus an ideal setting for an existential crisis of identity. Croydon! so drab, average and formica-clinical it offers no escape, no false flight of fantasy from who you are – no sudden jet-plane to the Marrakesh of the mind.

Added to which I have to confess that there *was* something fascinating in my absurd deception – was it some warped sense of authenticity? The lack of Kate's approval for my decision somehow making it more my own? A childish desire for exclusive possession of my own trivial fate? Despite all life's efforts to refashion me in the image of a man, sometimes I amaze myself with just how infantile a part of me remains. It is almost an achievement.

Of course, you don't have to change: there's no law against staying the same. I see it in people all around me: this dogged refusal to accept the obvious; this canine retention of the old bone of a marrow-less personality. Some like the taste of bone, I guess. Speaking personally, I had no choice. I *had* to change – and I could do that anywhere, couldn't I? Even somewhere – *especially somewhere* - as cheap and cheerless as Croydon.

## 119 – Lazarus entombed

Having, then, decamped to this suburban wasteland, the London SE20 of the mind - and deceived Kate - my immediate sensation was - ironically, given my proximity to them - one of disastrously painful distance from the people and things I loved, all of which only served to exaggerate my confusion. Surely it was madness to do what I was doing! To consciously decide to put oneself through this withdrawal from all known references, yet still remain within touching distance of them - like a junkie going cold turkey with the drugs still close to hand. – Ah but that at least was in the family genes!

'I'd ask you to keep the sound down on the TV in your room after ten o'clock as it disturbs the other guests!' declares my landlady with a voice like an air-raid siren.

'Breakfast is from 7.30 to 8.30! Sharp,' she adds, thus ruling out breakfast. Her expression in repose is one of a woman who has become terminally disenchanted with the human race as a result of its general untidiness. Looking at her blankly, I then think I hear her add "if there's anything else you want, keep it to yourself..." - but this might be my imagination. In my room I turn and look in the mirror and the face in it says to me: 'this is madness'.

Maybe conscious change involves a kind of descent in, through and out the other side of madness. Yes, that's why I'd come to Croydon – to go mad. In fact, the fact that I'd come to Croydon in the first place proved I was already mad!

Looking around at my four walls, I couldn't have chosen more suitable surroundings. That first afternoon I revelled in the desperate mediocrity of my B & B – this uber-typical one-room nightmare, this black hole in the suburban ground, this oubliette of consciousness where, as the first few hours rolled by inconspicuously, time threatened to devour me entirely – like that image by Goya of Saturn devouring his children. Now that I was here how was I to resist the great dark god of time? I had no strategy. Change, yes – but what precisely does that mean?

It is one thing to reject an old way of life, quite another to take up a new one. What do you do with your day? It is delivered to your door every morning, this square cardboard box containing nothing but the round hours you put in to it. How do you then square time's circle with nothing to do? Time is thus the most simultaneously rigid, shapeless and challenging gift of all. And it handed itself abundantly to me.

### 120 – The tomb of my B & B

'I'm sorry – I've closed the kitchen!' declares my landlady triumphantly at 8.31 am.

Sure enough, I have missed breakfast - so, too, next morning - and the next.

Traipsing back upstairs I began to find I had no answer to perhaps the profoundest of all existential questions: 'what makes you get out of bed?' And having no answer, I began to stay in bed. Perhaps I could just sleep away my angst? Perhaps this was why I had been drawn to Croydon's dismal tomb? 'To sleep, perchance to dream, to die, to sleep no more?' - Ah Shakespeare: consummate expert in the impossible art of solitude!

What then did I dream of? Trivia... of shallow social disharmonies, of being unprepared for dinner parties; of scurrying round a closing Waitrose, not being able to locate the Dauphinoise potatoes. Certainly I dreamt of nothing grand. I dreamt of no white horse.

Where was Pegasus in all of this? Where was the equine spirit of remembered inspiration? Gone. Mythical creatures from hot climates find it hard to settle in Croydon. Having dropped me off there, he had galloped away back to Mount Helicon and left me to consider my options. I had none - none but to pretend I was in Marrakesh.

### 121 – Lazarus un-risen.

After the first couple of days I stopped calling Kate, the Marrakesh pretence was too painful. Said I'd text instead; this thin substitute for communication involving less intense duplicity. Simple messages of reassurance – from a simpleton.

'Hope all good with you? How is the dear boy? How is Annette?' Tell me if you need me back. Everything fine here.'

Whereas, in truth, nothing was.

And maybe this was appropriate, because suddenly, without Kate and Tom, it was clear to me that I myself had died - *was* Lazarus – not raised from, but committed to the dead. The door to my room was the great stone that closed my tomb. As the second week began, I lived and walked, ate, slept and drank like a dead man. I *was* a dead man. The man I *had been* was nowhere to be seen.

Well, actually he was – but only in a thousand fragments all over my bedroom floor. Like a digital image of myself that had pixelated, frozen and then shattered in front of my very own eyes, 'I' had disintegrated again, but this time disastrously. What the hell was wrong with me?

Perhaps the question provided the answer. Hell. Hell was wrong with me. I had created a comfortable suburban version of it in my head.

The table in my room sported a couple of tattered, old copies of House and Gardens magazine – oddly enough, none of the ideal houses or gardens were in Croydon; the table also displayed one issue of 'Which' in which, predictably enough, German dishwashers triumphed – hidden beneath these was an old dictionary: I looked up the word' hell'. Apparently 'hell' stems from an Indo-European root meaning 'to cover, hide'. So in hell we are covered and hidden. Deprived of all contact with our fellows. Condemned. Denied social existence and acceptance. Left to rot – or burn – alone... in Croydon.

Yes, hell was what was wrong with me. I had literally become this neutral, dull room – its sterile emptiness was a one-lamp lightless leitmotif of me. Somehow I had allowed an experience as ecstatic as Auckland Avenue to degenerate, via a crap on Clapham Common, into this room in Croydon, which, with its soulless formica table, artificial flowers and artifice-less painting of a sunset upon the wall was the natural conclusion of the route I'd taken.

### 122 – I spy with my little eye.

In my second week pursuing my dead-end to its ultimate conclusion in Croydon, I followed another crazy route. I went and spied on Kate as she wheeled Tom in the nearby park.

I knew it would be painful – perhaps I did it *because* I knew it would be painful. Isn't this the soul of masochism? The conviction that one deserves punishment and derives pleasure from administering the perverse justice on oneself? So I went and spied on Kate. As I say, distance from those we love frames them with vital perspective - but also lends a stark objectivity to one's capacity to love.

There she was! Peering at her from a distance round a corner (I knew her times for venturing out with Tom) this frail woman – fragile not through any polemic of gender – but simply through the fact of being human and alone... with a young child: a condition my tediously repetitive disequilibrium had forced on them both - Tom, my son - who dares quantify a father's love for his son! There he is! There *she* is! Wheeling him, a small child in a pram across an expanse of green in a vast, impersonal metropolis. A blip of humanity in the flat-line of dead, urban indifference! How heroic is the simple fact of our humanity!

Then I suddenly saw Kate talking to a man – was he bothering her? What should I do if he was? Rush out, knock him out – and give Kate a heart attack into the bargain? He had an ice-cream – was he offering it to her? But no, she was OK. I thought I saw her laughing, and then they sauntered off - together.

I felt ashamed. And left too.

### 123 - Rimbaud

Why is it great men's thoughts come to mind when one is feeling small? Is there some inverse proportion relating humiliation to redemption? Staring at my room's battered formica table, suddenly, those wonderful words of Rimbaud from 'A Season in Hell' came back to haunt me: 'Ah once, if I remember well, my life was a feast at which all wines flowed...'

Where was that feast now? How, as I say, had the ecstasy of Auckland Avenue ended in the crap on Clapham Common? My time in Croydon was a fusty, foetid dining-table at which only poisonous, corked wines spilled. And so I drank them. Because they were all I had. The loss of meaning and value, the clichéd but nonetheless fatal loss of life's intoxication – the very reason to live: I began to drink the bitter wine of dispossession down to the lees. Because I was not here to feast but starve; to live, as I say, the living death of Lazarus... was that it? – But if so, to what end? *The* end? Thus, like Alice, but not in Wonderland, I wept a river of tears for my dead self.

It is said that a man crying is a harrowing sound – precisely because our gender, for whatever reasons, does it so rarely. It certainly disturbed my landlady.

'Are you all right in there?' The inquisitional tone of her demand shocked me out of my tears, just as, evidently, my mournful plaint had disturbed her indifference.

'I said – is everything OK? I heard someone crying... Is it just you, Mr Grant?'

So that's it! She thinks I've got someone in here with me! That I'm paying single occupancy for a double room – bless the English shopkeeper mentality! If you're going to have another person in there crying with you, then it's seventy-five pounds per night!

'No, no – just me... - I'm sorry.'

'Well, OK. I'm going out now, so I'd ask you to lock the door behind you if you go out too.'

'No, no – I'm staying in...' And I did – for days on end.

## *124 – Not depression*

Not depression. In depression one has no energy for grief; whereas mourning is dynamic, an active addiction: one consciously fuels it with one's tears. And I hit the bottle. Indeed, in Croydon my heart was bottle-shaped and I drank my own contents and cried them back out into the world and got swept away on intoxicating waves of grief. As I said: it is not easy to mourn your own passing. To survive one must be a good swimmer.

What are we but personality? Shorn of our habits, our emotional and reflective patterns – who are we? What do we do? When you get up every morning but can't hook back up into who you used to be; when you physically cannot pick up the threads of who you were - because the threads are electrified and will kill you with a thousand volts of unwanted memories - you have no place to hide - except Croydon....

So the second week shaded towards its end; hours bleached into each other. My room was like an abandoned back-office of a failed business. I was last year's sun-faded calendar no-one consulted anymore; my mind was littered with redundant thoughts like a floor strewn with belated, uncollected post.

Then, anachronistically shattering my oblivion, Kate's beaming face appears on my I-phone. I stare at it as the phone rings. Then my hand reaches out – and retracts itself. She leaves a message.

'Hope you're OK? All good here. Actually, Annette has invited me to go with her up North for a few days – you'll never guess where: bloody Lake District. Says she'll pay, which is bit embarrassing but I thought if you don't mind us not being here when get back... Anyway, let me know what you think...'

I'll tell you what I think: I think... I think I believe in reincarnation.

## 125 – Reincarnation and the landlady

It is one minute past ten.

'Can you please turn your TV down?' demands Mrs Ringwald, knocking on my door right on cue.

A day or so before I had asked my landlady about her German surname. Bad move. Her husband had deserted her several years before and gone back to the Black forest whence his tribe originated. Why had she kept the name, I wondered. Perhaps out of mutual respect for the Teutonic love of punctuality.

'Mr Grant, it's past ten o'clock!' she knocks again.

Suddenly I threw the door open and confronted Mrs Ringwald – with a request to join me in the programme I was watching: its subject, reincarnation. Taken aback she offered no resistance.

'Do you believe in it, Mrs Ringwald?' I asked. 'Because I think it's a question of belief not science.' I sat her down.

'Don't know as I do,' she replied, like a character from a post-war John Mills film.

'My point is that reincarnation, 'rebirth' 're-becoming – whatever you want to call it ---'

'Metempsychosis!' added Mrs Ringwald adroitly.

'Pardon ---?'

'The transmigration of souls!'

'Yes – can hardly be proven. But once you *do* decide to believe in it, all sorts of things start to make poetic sense, Mrs Ringwald; even my being here, in Croydon, at your B & B!' Mrs Ringwald pondered my hypothesis.

'I *do* believe that science is a kind of religion, actually,' she eventually offered up. 'I mean, how many scientists actually see quantum theory in operation? I'll tell you how many – none.'

I had to agree.

'It may be logical – but it's still conjecture!' she declared.

'And as such occupies the realm of abstraction,' I confirmed.

'And one can only live life theoretically for so long before taking leave of one's marbles – rather like you Mr Grant! – Goodnight!' She rose and quit my room in a Scarlet O'Haran swirl of red silk.

'Ah goodnight, Mrs Ringwald: bright lady of my dark night! Soft maiden of companionable delight! Goodnight sweet fantasy....'

### 126 – If it were true

You see, if reincarnation is true (I thought to myself, lying on my bed some time after Mrs Ringwald's departure, like a corpse suddenly reanimated by the mysterious re-emergence of some spark of hope), it makes sense of everything. If reincarnation is true, maybe I brought Auckland Avenue and Clapham Common down on myself; maybe in a past life I could have been somebody who practised meditation in which a sense of self ecstatically diminishes! But maybe this person was also actually no saint. Maybe, when not meditating, he or she drank a lot, or whored or was a whore - or gambled – or worked in The City - wherever that 'city' then was. Maybe he or she was someone whose desires were riven in two, with the effect that they experienced the opposing forces of human consciousness within the same personality. Isn't that possible: don't bad men and women sometimes perform inexplicably good acts? I could see how patterns of cause and effect might work within the confines of one life… but carrying over into another life altogether?

Maybe the problem requires a leap, not just of faith, but of imagination. Might we not imagine our disembodied personalities leaping over the vast nocturnal lacuna of death and carrying on into the next life, like an electric spark leaping between two nodes! Is this so fanciful? Actually, isn't there something fanciful about the laws of physics? The very fact that the spark does leap, *needs* to leap from one node to another? It's as if energy is primary and always seeks some physical form to attach itself to. In the same way as the spark, then, couldn't the life-force leap between physical bodies *just because it is desperate to do so?* And so what if all this *is* somewhat fanciful! Are we really so prosaic, so lacking in imagination as to need things to be proven by reason all the time?

## 127 – My love affair with the spirit of thoughts

I didn't know it, but in this way, towards the end of my short but seemingly endless time in Croydon another change was taking place, another love affair reaching its conclusion. I picked up a text from Kate.

'How are the markets in Marrakesh? Don't come home without being ripped off. Tom loves the mountains – and the hotel scrambled egg. When do you get home? Let me know? Thinking of you. XXX'

'Thinking of you...'

What is this power of thought that can cross mountains and seas? That can exalt or desolate?

And then the thought occurred that, ironically, Croydon, in its ultra-averageness, was a kind of imaginal matrix that drove one to fantasise, precisely to escape its uber-dependable banality.

Ah the self-regenerative power of thought that never quits us! Not whether we're good, bad or indifferent, sick or well; infantile or senile; wherever we are, in heaven or hell, Paris or....

In Croydon all I had was thoughts – and feelings, which I then thought about. They did not need me to think them up, these thoughts: they had a life of their own; came whether I bade them or not. Certainly, I know not whence they came or whose, in effect, they were.

They turned up, as I say, uninvited in my mind, like gate-crashers at a party with no people, so that, with no loyalty to me, they quickly left again, sticking around only long enough to tell me I was mad, but also the sanest person they had ever met: - thoughts that wished me well, or scowled behind my back; thoughts that reminded me of family members and associated loyalties; thoughts that told of treacheries; thoughts that flattered me, made eyes at me; thoughts that told me I should come over and see them sometime; thoughts that ridiculed me and said I should seek help; honey-tongued thoughts that coupled with me like Aphrodite, black thoughts that, like Medusa, froze my blood; political thoughts that sought to enlist my support; dispossessed thoughts like hungry ghosts that starved on false truths and wanted me to starve with them; thoughts that laughed at me and cried with me... thoughts. Who knew what they were or what they wanted from me.

One afternoon in Croydon I turned on them and asked... or, I should say, one particular thought - itself more prominent, powerful and loquacious than all the other thoughts - asked on my behalf. This same thought stood up in the madhouse of my mind and declaring itself supervisor of all other lesser thoughts, asseverated that it would now be directing their affairs. Thus this one thought began to dominate proceedings.

'Nobody is leaving here,' said this thought, 'until one question's answered.'

'What's that?' clamoured all the other assembled thoughts.

'You know what it is!'

'No we don't! We don't!' they cried.

'What is the way back to life – any life? In which direction does it lie?'

'That's two questions!' chirped some wise-guy 'thought' at the back of the hall. The supervisor-thought ignored this facetiousness.

'No-one is leaving here, no-one is even getting out of bed until we have an answer to that question! When – and only when – that question's receives an answer, we will roll away the stone and get Lazarus out of here...'

### 128 – The insomniac's dream

It is rumoured that Hamlet himself once passed through Croydon on a tour of England in 1464. Nothing much has changed. Nor would the prince of melancholia have been noticed had he arrived last week. Indeed, with his propensity for dark dreams he would have found himself at home in Mrs Ringwald's. We could've shared insomnia, the personal hell of the switched-on light, the mind that will not shut down, that fails to respond to the need for sleep, that stays, like a crashed computer, locked on to a programme that is not responding, that will never respond. Insomnia, the perfection of futility! Neither rest, nor sleep, nor creativity, but some dim limbo in between where the soul floats aimlessly and unconnectedly, searching for its raison d'être. - Ah Hamlet, doomed to supply the face and portrait of the Western soul for all eternity!

In the end, and speaking personally, I slept, of course. Morpheus, the god of sleep, loves to play the trickster role using the persona of insomnia. Depriving you of sleep for hours on end, he then plies you at the last moment with a sleep so deep you struggle to wake at all; and when you do emerge from this sleep's marine depths it is at the behest of a giant wave of a dream that thrashes you upon its shore. So it was at the end of that particularly insomniac night in Croydon, as I accidentally fell headlong into deep sleep and got caught inside the submarine vortex of a dream.

I was walking close to the fatal beauty of Beachy Head (which I happened to have visited recently, with no self-malice aforethought, I hasten to add), and a little boy bicycled past me towards the cliff edge – purposeful and unafraid.

I reached out and caught him as his bike careered over the cliff. Asking him if was OK, the boy had suddenly become a man and turned to address *me* like a father:

'Thank you. By the way, the answer to your question is simple: - "this cliff-edge..."'

I felt vaguely offended by the insouciance of the revelation.

'This cliff-edge is where you live.'

I said nothing, *could* say nothing.

'So don't try to walk away. Forget your name, your home; forget desire, remorse. Anywhere you go will lead back here.... This edge, this sky, this point-of-view, of no return... is *you*. Then he looked past me.

'You're lucky living with these sea-views...'

I turned to look and then turned back - but he had gone. Further off a boy was bicycling away at speed.

### 129 – Notice to quit

The morning after the dream, I knew my time in Croydon was done, my sentence served. I woke in an alarming state of peace. Overnight Croydon's spell of oblivion was self-evidently broken. I had awoken as if from illness, from the throes of fever newly past. That fever was grief. How, I know not, but the dream had cleansed me of most of its debilitating poison. I no longer mourned for my dead self. On the contrary, that morning, on getting up and opening the windows in my B & B, I committed the ashes of my dead self to the winds.

As I cast my eyes around my bedroom it no longer possessed the hallucinatory proportions of a prison but those of a small suburban room I didn't like very much. Thus, not needing to stay a moment longer, I resolved to pack and leave without a moment's notice. As for Mrs Ringwald - let landladies the world over keep their deposits! Thus, on Thursday afternoon, I signed no receipt, on no dotted line, but simply quit.

# Part four --- Ascent

## 130 – Flocks of wild parrots in London

True to her word, Kate was not back when I returned. Without her and Tom; untenanted by love, the house disowned itself of any relevance in my life. So in those disinherited days I did the simplest thing – and walked away from it. Miles away. Every day. Across London....

- Walked from grief to its calm opposite, contentment; and from East to West across London. I always ended up in Richmond, near the 'great park'.

There are flocks of wild parrots in this wealthy suburban reach of London, this green neck of its asphalt woods. Suddenly emerging from the unseen into the seen, they fleck the dawn and dusk with minor, meteoric streaks of green. Hundreds of them Jackson-Pollocking our grey capital in the colours of their paradise, re-interpreting it in the name of a spirit perhaps never before seen. Purposeless, unconfined delight....

The parrots, we hear, escaped from pet cages over the decades, gradually establishing themselves in the climate, laying claim to an exotic, indeed, quixotic existence in a cageless capital of suburban sky wherein they now thrive and whence they threaten to invade London's concrete heart.

I would go to a particular spot and just watch them fly around my head – like St Francis without the holiness. I liked the parrots' utter impossibility, the fact of their profoundly happy inappropriateness. They were both in

238

and out-of-place. And thus, birds of a feather, they flew, the tutelary spirits of my new state of mind. To this day I cannot bear to see any bird caged: the hands, old or young, that set them there, and the voices that coo, though their love be couched in sentimental terms, never can be kind.

When I rang Kate for the first time in three weeks, to arrange for her and Tom's return from The Lakes, for some reason - no doubt, my lie, as yet undisclosed - I had prepared myself for anger.

'So you're still alive then?' she joked with a gentle verve that somehow disconcerted me. It was a tone that had been absent from her voice for far too long. In the background I heard French being spoken – always a pleasant sound for me.

A day or two later when I picked her and Tom up from St Pancras their appearance on the platform (Annette was continuing on up to Scotland) disarmed me and my eyes welled up with tears.

What is guilt at its best? A powerful force for atonement, a positive desire for expiation: the removal of an obstacle that lies in the way of shared happiness. Having rolled away the stone and risen Lazarus-like from my tomb in Croydon, there was now another standing stone to move between Kate and me. And it was heavier than my stupid lie.

On getting home, Kate seemed to take inordinately long unpacking. I turned round to call upstairs.

'Kate - your tea! --- Oh I didn't see you there...' She had been standing in the doorway.

'Matt... it's... I want.... Don't be cross ---'

'What do you mean?'

'I need to tell you something.'

'What?' In my necessary orgy of self-obsession in Croydon I had forgotten other people have lives and that they too might have tales to tell.

'It sounds stupid... it *is* stupid.'

'What is?'

'I told Annette not to... I told her there was no point in him coming over....'

'What?

'With her - to England... I mean.'

'Who? What are you talking about?'

'Nothing.' A pause. 'You haven't told me a thing about Marrakesh. You don't look very brown!'

'No, I... stayed in the shade.... How is Annette by the way?'

'Fine.'

'Is she coming back down? After Scotland, I mean...'

'Maybe. Yes... no.... I don't know ---'

'I mean, will I see her? I haven't seen her for.... Don't tell me she's avoiding me....'

'No!'

'Then why doesn't she ---'

'I've slept with someone.'

'What?'

'I said I've...'

"Slept with someone." The sentence sounded like a foreign language. Like French. Indeed, apparently his name was Alain - old-fashioned somehow – even in French. A friend of Annette's husband who had accompanied them all up North. Actually he was fifteen years older than Kate. But a decade or so is not long in the life of a sun, and he was evidently the source of the sunlight in her voice.

'I met him when I went over – that time when you...'

'Yes, I remember...' If I sounded distracted it was because I was still mentally brushing off my French, which had been very good at school but which had, like my capacity to love, become very rusty.

'I'm sorry,' said Kate.

'Why?' I asked.

And I meant it. Why should she be sorry? Unless, she hadn't enjoyed it. I mean. I'm not affecting saintliness; it just seemed the natural question to ask, given that the brief affair had so obviously lightened dark days for her. Then I thought 'brief..?'

'Do you love him?' I asked, reading woodenly from the rejected lover's script.

'Of course not... he's just a friend,' she replied, turning the page. 'We all drank too much wine...'

Then Kate must've mistaken my practise of the subjunctive of silence for an accusative inflexion.

'Actually, you know what: I'm not sorry,' she added: 'It's been tough, Matt, with you, these last few months.'

The assertion needed no proof. If I had found living with myself impossible, it took no great leap of imagination to see that, at one remove from my self-interest, Kate had found living with me unbearable.

'What do you want to do?' I asked with intractable reasonableness.

'What I *am* doing.'

'What's that?'

'Standing here, drinking tea with you – with Tom upstairs.'

Of course, our now one-and-a-bit year-old now chose this moment to wake from the briefest of sleeps. Indeed, he'd reached the strangely horrifying age of toddlerdom wherein his daytime sleeps had all but disappeared.

'I'll go up,' said Kate. Though she had stopped breast-feeding a month or two back, it was still her instinct to be first on the scene at Tom's distressed waking.

'No, let me.'

And with that almost meaningless, momentary role-reversal of parental generosity, a subtle shift occurred in my relationship with Kate.

Later that day, our mutual confessions progressed. I told Kate about Marrakesh. At first Kate laughed; then it came out how I had spied on her at the park: the man offering her the almost comically unseasonal ice-cream had of course been Alain. Thus, slowly the evidence of the shared distance in our relationship added a darker context. So we talked. And talked. We talked to an absurd degree – as disaffected lovers do – in our attempt to turn back time. And we did turn it back a bit.

I told Kate about my love of Croydon. She inquired with her customary detachment and objectivity and perhaps a hint of acid - 'What did you expect? It's a suburban shithole.'

I told Kate that if my dream of the cliff and the boy with the bike had meant anything it was that I had to accept that I was no longer a child; that to be fully human is somehow to accept - no - *embrace* the dangerous reality of the present moment: the fact that you are only alive right now.

– *'Only?'* Why do I use that word? How long is now? 'Now' is all there is. - Ever. Now is eternal because it's always here. We are a conduit for life's electricity. We are lightning conductors: life strikes us, passes through us into the earth and we are the earth we stand upon.

Where *is* our permanence? Are our feelings even ours? If they are, why can't we command them to appear when we want, bend them to our will? Well, we try, and the harder we hang onto them the more ethereally they elude our grasp. There is nothing so dead as the purple, paradisiacal butterfly pinned upon the lepidopterist's baize.

That night Kate rejected Alain. Ruthlessly, as she lay in my arms, I thought of him - and shed no tears.

244

## 131 – Next morning

There's always a next morning – there *has* to be. It's the proof of all the theorising of the night before; whether it works or not, whether it can be brought down off the blackboard – and translated into life.

I got up before Kate; she needed to sleep – and, released from the schizophrenic insomnia and listlessness of Croydon, I needed *not* to; and then Tom was already awake, of course. I brought him downstairs, made a bit of breakfast and gave him his Lego and looked at him making sense of the out-size bricks. He was old enough to stick the extra-large bits together into some shape – any shape. Then he shook them apart and threw them across the floor. Like lovers do with love that doesn't fit – or just because they can.

How strange to love! To not be satisfied with one's own being, to feel the need to reach out and weave another person into the tapestry of oneself! We are the warp and weft of each other's desire. We complete each other's pattern.

What then of the pattern of solitude? Hadn't Auckland Avenue taught me that the most extraordinary thing can happen – can only happen - in solitude? Then maybe love is another - shared - way into Auckland Avenue? But - and sexual ecstasy apart - given that it is almost a banality to observe that love dissolves two into one, dissolves personality into an experience, however brief, of consummate contentment - at what point or moment does my isolation merge into love's all-consuming unity? Where do 'I' end and 'you' begin? We do _we_ begin?

'What do you say, Tom?' he looked at me quizzically. 'Which colour bricks do you like best? The red? For me it's red.' And I started to make a shape for Tom, which, giggling, he unmade as quickly as I pieced it all together.

Are we Lego? In fitting neatly together our bodies certainly seem to say so. But if we are drawn together in a thought or kiss, or love and friendship's bliss, surely this is only possible because, in reality, we have no hard edges. Can marble melt? Surely this dissolution of two (or more) souls into one is only possible because we are essentially Protean in nature: shape-shifting water gods who flow into one another, like delta rivers into a sea. What is love if not an extinction of selfhood, an ecstatic drowning in oceanic union, a discovery that we can breathe underwater, an extinction that we thus desperately desire?

Indeed, are we not, in this sense, always trying to extinguish ourselves in love? Without love, don't we experience our 'selves' as painfully separate, experience separation as painful? Why? Because selfhood _is_ inherently painful, an experience of isolation, of distance and acute vulnerability. Isn't the keynote of this life one of disharmonious fracture, of divorce from every object of desire, found in sensations as trivial as the thirst for a cup of tea to the tormenting hunger of loneliness and the thirst for love?

246

But why, if this is the case, does love always lead to disillusionment? Perhaps because, in seeking to merge with any object of desire, we carry within us too much that is still indissoluble? Perhaps romance is still too full of solid egotism – with too much that is also indissoluble in the object of our love? Perhaps romance itself is too viscous, and not fluid enough to pass entirely through the walls of selfhood. Perhaps, to flow freely and be entirely communicable, love needs to be utterly free of all impurities - both in the lover and the beloved. Didn't someone say that the object of devotion dissolves all that is impure in the devotee? Perhaps we understand nothing of this kind of love yet.

## 132 – Couples

And so, of course, Kate and I got back together.

Because that's what certain, not-unsuited couples do. That's why they separate – so that they can get back together again and mend the damage, in the hope that the repair works better than the original. Doesn't a broken bone knit together stronger than before? In this sense, there did indeed seem to be something more real about the way that we related to each than before – more real - and less dependent.

Indeed, the first phase of all relationships lasts three years. People fall in love; the thrill wears off after eighteen months - because that's how long it takes to get to know a lover on the superficial basis of his/her habits, good, bad or indifferent; of the rhythm of their moods, what you will accept, what you can't take, et cetera, et cetera. The second eighteen months are the cooling off period when you gradually get sick of each other. It begins, of course, with silly arguments and childish lovers' tiffs, graduating imperceptibly to the real, barely muted, existential nausea at the appearance of the other in the room. Sometimes you'd like to kill them, throw them quickly in an acid bath and have done with it, but this would be uncivil. No, the exit from the love affair is a very definite pas-de-deux that requires a deftness, even a kind of skill in its conduct if the dance is to lead you both neatly to the exit door without unnecessary public embarrassment and/or too many toes crushed in the proceedings.

Then, after you have separated and tried out one or two other lovers and found them wanting too, gradually, usually during a lean period, your thoughts turn back to the first one that worked better than the rest. OK, it wasn't perfect, but you're no longer eighteen, or twenty-one or even twenty-five (that age of the unsung quarter-life crisis!) you no longer expect Miss or Mr Right to walk into your room with a rose between their teeth – and if they did you'd quite rightly ring social services. No, you're in your early thirties, way past the 11$^{th}$ hour of youth, and it's very much time to get serious.

So Kate and I accepted each other's imperfections. She knew my strengths and weaknesses: that I was an essentially good humoured, mild-mannered, albeit slightly skittish man prone to the odd – extremely odd – un-drug-assisted hallucinogenic altered state now and again. But all that was, I could now assure her, a known quantity; I had a handle on it; had a handle on this window onto another world that lay beyond our third floor flat. And I could close that window when necessary - even when it flew open of its own accord.

But then, of course, there was the money. There's *always* the money. Or the lack of it.

Nothing has changed. Tomorrow morning I'm due back behind the wheel of my bus.

'You can't go back – I won't let you go back.' Kate declares.

'I need to sort things out... what happened on the Common; if I don't serve out a period of notice they'll just stop my pay. Believe me, I won't stay a moment longer than I have to....

Later that day I go upstairs and open the wardrobe: there it is: my uniform – hanging in the closeted dark like a gibbeted, boneless corpse: surely I can't inhabit it again, revive this dead man's life? Suddenly it looks like a clown's outfit – all outsize lapels and silly angles. Then let me wear it as one for the last few weeks! Let me turn the joke upon the job that has reduced me to tears.

### 133 – Nothing happens....

Next day my first shift back begins after lunch. I catch a quick word with Donna in the canteen. She gives me a great hug. It is strangely moving to stumble upon the wonderful oasis of her humanity again. I hadn't realised how much Donna already meant to me amidst the depot's mire of mediocrity.

'Where the hell've you been, you little truant!'

'Nowhere – well, I nearly went to Marrakesh actually.'

'Oh and did you nearly have a good time? I nearly slept with Brad Pitt last week myself. Jesus when I look back at the all the things I've nearly done, I've nearly had a hell of a life!'

'Yeah, well I really ended up in a B & B in Croydon!'

'Wise decision – so much more exotic than Morocco! Tell me about it later! When does your shift end?' calls out Donna as she leaves to go to her bus. We arrange to meet later.

Typically, nothing much has changed at the depot: the patterns of human behaviour are all the same. Drivers don't talk much except to exchange predictable comments and mutual consolations about politics, pop-stars, bomb-scares and the like. Certainly no-one makes any mention of my forced exposure and evacuation upon Clapham common.

So I get into my bus and turn around to look at the ghosts of the passengers whose stares haunt the memory of what I had to do in broad daylight that day upon the Common. As yet, it appears I've had no notice of any complaint, official or otherwise, about my Clapham Common antics... have I, then, got clean away with it?

### 134 – Ronnie and the return to The Square Mile

Strangely, driving out of the depot that afternoon, I felt protected by a sense of my own posthumousness: whether the word exists, the mood most certainly does: that state of mind where, having died, life cannot harm you. And I had died – at least the bus driver in me had – and with him my fear of the job. Not that I drove my bus without anxiety; rather that, knowing my days in the bus were numbered, I could regulate their stress more effectively than at any time in the past year or so. I was somehow put back in a measure of control. That said, the god of circumstance never sleeps for long.

As if to mark the internal change, an external alteration also occurs: I am put on a new route I know all too well, a route that takes me back through The City – the irony is so large I cannot escape it for a moment during my drive along the Square Mile's streets. Like a criminal returning to the scene of the crime, I drive my bus past St Paul's, along Cheapside, Threadneedle Street, right back into the heart of my modest malfeasance at the bank. Glancing up I see my old office windows. And it all looks so respectable....

Ah this ethical Bermuda Triangle in which integrity mysteriously goes missing. This 'Square Mile' of moral smoke and mirrors, this glass concourse of transient transactions where the only real stock and lasting currency is debt? I drive my bus right through and all I see is men and women disappearing into, and emerging from, windowed buildings. One of them is Ronnie who invisibly emerges from my past and gets on my bus as I enter Lombard Street. Ronnie, of course, had always made a point of never using public transport - said it was demeaning to all who used it. I now knew what he meant.

How we laughed at our changed circumstances! Only we didn't. He stood there dumbfounded. He had only recognised me on looking up when, questioning the tenner in his hand, I asked him if he had anything smaller.

'That's a bit personal, driver!'

'That's my Ronnie!'

'Jesus H Christ! What the fuck....'

'Language, Ronnie, there are civilised human beings on board...' I motion Ronnie to stand aside as other passengers got on board, then, as we started off, I headed Ronnie off at the pass.

'It's temporary, Ronnie....'

'I should fuckin' hope so! Bus driver – are you mad? Seriously! What's happened to you? Last thing I heard you'd joined the foreign legion.'

'That was last week. This week it's buses. Next week, submarines.'

'Yeah, very funny. Seriously mate – what happened? I mean I know what happened…'

'Do you, I don't', the irony escaped him.

'Look, if you need a favour. There's always an opening somewhere. I'll keep my ear out, see what I can do.'

'Thanks, Ronnie.'

'This is my stop, mate.'

'I thought you never used the buses, Ronnie?'

'I don't; there's a girl I'm trying to avoid. She waits for me at Mansion House – I think she's stalking me. Don't laugh. It's true. Look, Catch you later!'

And with that, Ronnie had leapt off the platform, never to be seen again, except by the girl, whom, I was soon to hear, he later got a court order against. She was not to come within a hundred yards of Ronnie. Conversely, I thought, equality of justice should also have stated that Ronnie was not to come within a hundred yards of any woman....

## 135 – Nemesis

And suddenly the axe falls. No, I have not 'got clean away' with the event on Clapham Common. Back at the bus depot there is a bizarre surprise awaiting me – of the moral variety.

And, indeed, a bus depot, with all its base materials and discarded containers, is a good place to explore the wasteland of moral dubiety. The moment you drive a bus back into a depot you not only decommission your sense of purpose, but also divest yourself of a sense of stress as physical as a suit of armour. Parked up in the shadows, the buses become so much dead, red metal. Drivers unbutton collars and ties, get ready to change back into human beings – or what's left of them. Some may have only a few hours off before returning to do it all again; others may face the glorious luxury of the long weekend rota when they clock off late on a Thursday night and don't come back to drive until Monday afternoon.

Others still, such as me, may open their locker and find an adult incontinence pad with a photo pinned to it, both hung from the inside of the locker door. In the photo a man in a high-vis jacket, possibly a bus driver squatting, taking what looks, to all undeniable intents and purposes, like a dump in the full glare of public view on a common in London. Scrawled on the photo, I read a ludicrously badly spelt threat...

## 136 - Bad apple

'Is that for real?' jeers the voice over my shoulder in the locker room, as I stare at the photo of me palpably not 'being excused' on Clapham Common...

'What is it? What's that bloke doing behind that tree? Let's 'ave a butcher's.'

Big Len goes to snatch the photo from me but I slam the locker door and tell him politely to fuck off.

Big Len, my erstwhile instructor, is one of those six billion people you instinctively dislike on first meeting them.... But, seriously, we all know them: certain folk have a distinct look in their eye which tells you they won't come at you directly, but prefer the round-the-corner diversion via cunning and insinuation. Big Len, prime amongst them, has always been an Alpha male of innuendo.

He wishes me well, "Fuck you too," and goes off into the night. I open the locker again and tentatively read the childish felt-tip writing on the photo of me crouched behind the Clapham Common tree:

'Remember that movee, "I know what you did last sumer..." – How much is the orijanul of this picher worth?'

Incredulous, I read the message on the photo again:

"How much is the orijanul of this picher worth?''

So bizarre are the implications that it takes more than a few moments to take the seriously.

Blackmail? In a bus depot in Catford?

Then again - what better place?

'He knows what I did last summer...' You're kidding me, right? You're telling me, whoever you are, that you're trying to blackmail me - me! For money? I'm a bus driver - like you for Chrissake – haven't you noticed? No, it must be a joke. Yes, that's it: this bloke – whoever he is - is threatening to tell everyone at the depot for a laugh - not money. Still... What does he want me to do..? And who is he? Where is he? Maybe he's taking another picture of me right now?

### 137 – Blind Man's buff

How does one regulate one's own capacity for suspicion? Unmodulated, suspicion turns you round and round until you are the befuddled moral centre of your own game of ethical blind man's buff....

I survey the faces at the depot canteen: old lags proudly lined up in positions of seniority nearest to the tea-urn, jealously guarding their status in the battalion of veterans formed specially for dead-end lives. Woe betide you if you should inadvertently sit in a seat allotted for someone of far weightier rank!

Who the fuck is my ridiculous blackmailer?

Maybe old Ted over there? Benign old bugger with nothing on his mind except retirement, and no malice in his heart except for his wife's sister who 'had always tried to poison her against him...' – Poison! Was Ted capable of another kind of poison? Real moral poison? Was Ted trying to blackmail me? Or perhaps it actually was Big Len, the instructor, who had merely feigned interest in the note – having written it himself? Had I had the cruelly ironic misfortune to crap in front of his binocularised eyes that day on Clapham Common? Or was it Big Len's fellow instructor, Simple Simon, the disgusting, bloated pie-man – never somehow seen without one in his tubby, grubby mits? Was he the hidden dragon to my crouching tiger behind that Clapham tree? Was he fondling photos of me even now along with some godforsaken beef and onion pie..?

Which of these unmitigatedly average individuals was it who knew what I'd done last summer? Which? Ah there's Donna! ..... Not Donna, who over the months has become a good friend? Maybe as a joke...? No, don't be absurd. Don't even go there.

### 138 – Who?

That night I get home so late after my shift that Kate is asleep. Nor is she awake early next morning when I begin another at 7.30am. So I leave her a note on the breakfast table.

'All good at the depot. I'm being blackmailed, as you would expect. Someone apparently has pictures of 'what I did last summer' on Clapham Common. Don't worry, will sort it out with Clever Clive. Speak soon.'

First person I bump into at the depot is Donna. Over a canteen tea I tell her the truth about Clapham Common, and sound her out about the identity of my blackmailer.

'Fock knows – could be any one of the tossers in this place – though my money's on Big Len. Only 'cos I can't stand him, mind!' Then Donna changes tack to what she considers more serious matters.

'Jesus, why didn't you tell me you're ill. Are you seeing the doctor? Take time off for Chrissake!'

'I <u>have</u> taken time off.'

'Well take some more! Look, if there's anything I can do to help? Well of course there isn't! But if there is, you let me know. I mean it.'

Donna then has to begin her shift, for which she's already made herself late by listening to my ludicrous story. The dignity with which she has done so, especially in the light of her own far greater concerns, shames the germ of suspicion that only a day before had sprouted in the sunless shadows of my sickly conscience.

So before my shift I stride into Clever Clive's office – much to his surprise.

'Hallo Matt, I didn't know we had a meeting planned...'

'Clive,' I state nonchalantly. 'Someone's got a key to my locker.'

'What?' inquires Clive, barely looking up from his desk; thus disarming my contrived equanimity.

'Someone's broken into my locker.'

'Broken in - how?'

'Not broken in exactly. Someone with a key has put something in my locker – I was wondering if you knew anything about it.'

'Why would I know anything about it'; he looks up at last. 'What is it they've put in there? If that fuckin' idiot Jim's been up to his tricks with chicken giblets again... stunk the place out for a month last time!

'No, no it's not chicken giblets....'

'Has anything gone missing?'

'No, nothing's gone missing.'

'Good. Playing silly buggers is one thing; but I will not have thieves in my depot: there I draw the line! I'll get the law in. Do you want me to get the law in, 'cos I will!'

Suddenly I realise Clever Clive has nothing to do with it.

'No, no, thanks Clive, I'll deal with it.... I just thought you ought to know...'

Then as I'm quitting his drab, 'to-do' littered, directive-strewn world Clever Clive calls out: 'Try the janitor! Phil's the only one with a master key...'

So he is... - Phil... you absolute fucker.

### 139 – Back on board with Lola

Next morning I drove out of the depot more in amazement than distress.

It was inevitable of course: things come in three's: odd events, signs, tall dark strangers, old friends, lovers, blackmailers, Ronnie... Lola. When you *want* to meet them, you don't; conversely, when they are the last people in the world you want to set eyes on, there they are, standing shamelessly before you. Fate is a callously brilliant impresario, he brings utterly disparate people and circumstances together and makes perfect theatre of them.

Thus it was with a barely contained sense of humiliation that I received Lola on board my bus that unsuspecting Thursday afternoon. "of all the gin joints, in all the towns, etc, etc". There she stood. Only for a few moments. But a few moments constitute an eternity when embossed upon the soul by the hot metal of embarrassment.

'Matt!' Lola flashed those relentlessly dark eyes at me; dark eyes in the depths of whose intimate recesses I had once lost myself, like a cave-explorer lost in primitive ecstasies of semiotic-erotic discovery. Once again, my light seemed small in the face of her softly penetrable shadow and I could see only the ghosts of our shared past as passengers queued up behind Lola.

'Matt!' She called my name again, as if bringing rescue to someone lost and injured in those same depths. Did she mean me?

I turned to look, but there was no-one else called Matt driving the bus: yes, she meant me. So I owned up to the crime of my identity – and called back to the echo in her depths.

'Lola! How are you?'

'I'm all right.'

A pause.

'Actually, I'm pregnant.'

Where the truth was concerned, Lola had always been blunt and bald – rather like the baby she was apparently soon to have.

'Pregnant? Who by?' I shot back with Sherlock Holmesian acuity.

For some reason, Lola looked confused.

'Not… not Ronnie..?'

'Christ, do me a favour!'

'Of course, sorry.'

Then a voice from the queue.

'Driver, can we get the fuck on board, please?'

Lola stood awkwardly to the side as Old Street's unrepentantly unromantic travellers pushed past, both her – and our chance-rekindled liaison.

Lola – pregnant! If not by Ronnie, then by whom? 'Whom' such a lovely old-fashioned word, rhymes with room, tomb, catacomb – and womb…. Then the thought absurdly dawns.

'Me?'

'What?' inquires Lola as the bus's background rush of impersonal noise seeks to crush our platform intimacy.

'Is it me?'

'Is what you?'

'You said....'

'What? O for god's sake, Matt! Yes, it's you: the baby has taken two years to gestate!'

'Oh God, look I'm really sorry, Lola, I'm a little confused at the moment.'

'Shouldn't you be keeping your social life to your spare time, driver?' inquires another passenger, throwing metal coins into my receptacle.

'How did this happen?' Lola asks, gazing with uncertain compassion at my confinement in the driver's cabin.

'It's a long story. I'll tell it to you some day.'

Then, by way of excusing myself from the dialogue, I made the terrible error of inviting Lola for a drink, which mistake she compounded by accepting. There's a reason why paths diverge, why some people occupy the hinterland of your past: they harmonise with the set of circumstances, both emotional and physical, that pertain to that particular time in your life; conversely, to drag them out of that period drama and try and make them fit somewhere else in the plot of your contemporary tragicomedy does them a grave disservice. Robbed of the talents to amuse or shock which they possessed in the past, stripped of that particular script, of their specific movements upon that historic stage, they flounder like third-rate actors confused by your miserably inept direction.

Thus it is that Lola and I plan to meet up a week later....

### 140 – Not messing around

Another shift ends – another photo pinned inside my locker.

"I'm not messing arownd. If you don't wanna see this picher on the owtside of your locker – and all rownd the depo - tell me what it's werth! If not, I'm shore the police wil be interested in enee infermashun about a man exposin himself on Clapham Common. Leeve me yor mobile number on the picher and we'l speak layter."

Immediately I go round to Phil the Janitor's hide-out at the back of the depot, only to find it's his day off.

Back home, Kate scrutinises the photo as incredulously as I did originally; though the source of her disbelief seems to be mainly one of style.

'Why didn't you take off your high-vis jacket ferfuxake? – when you had to go, I mean?'

'Shit, you're right – I'll remember next time!' My sarcasm does the trick. She laughs.

'I can't take this seriously!'

264

'No, but what if he *does* tell the police?'

'Tell them the truth – you were ill, for chrissake! Anyway, he won't do that, the fucker's bluffing!'

Ah, yes 'the truth'; there's always that. Moving in a social environment of repressed fears and anxiety for so long I had forgotten how disarming and powerful the simple truth could be. In my confrontation with Phil the Janitor I will be armed with it.

### 141 – Son of Lola

So Lola and I meet up and it doesn't go like clockwork: we don't laugh about old times, we don't get drunk, don't lose definition and don't, for obvious reasons, fall into bed with each other. For both of us life, once a situation-comedy of optionally enjoyable proportions, has unaccountably become all too serious. And we can't change channels.

'Good to see you Matt. I always felt we... always felt I....'

'Good to see you too Lola.' A pregnant pause ensues – mainly because Lola *is* pregnant.

'So when's the amazing event?'

'Mid-to-late October – around the 20th, they say.'

'Ah, a Libra – cracking good sign! Never knew a Libra I didn't like! Balanced characters. Good at friendship.'

'Since when were you interested in astrology?'

'Since this morning. Read it in The Sun: "at the end of this week my financial affairs are set for a massive upturn!" – which gives the prediction about two hours to come true. '

'It *is* Ronnie,' Lola interrupts me casually.

'Sorry?'

'So am I.'

My mind relapses into a swamp of stupidity from which I haul myself out with the question:

'*What* is Ronnie?'

'The father... of this....' She confesses, hardly looking down at the impending change in her bodily geography.

'Ronnie? But you said --- '

'I know what I said.... I don't know how it happened. Well, actually, I do: - the way it always happens with Ronnie.'

I don't know what to say. Lola takes the hint and prompts my indignation.

'I had to get a court order – for a paternity test. You know what Ronnie's like.'

I still didn't know what to say, so Lola feeds my line.

'Ronnie's a cunt,' she avers incontrovertibly.

'He's the last man I'd want as the father of my child! But he ought to pay something – he can afford to pay something – he *should* pay something!'

'He should pay through the bloody nose!' I rejoin, my professional sense of umbrage suddenly back in gear.

'Can you believe: he took a court order out against me when I tried to talk to him about it. Said I was stalking him! I had to spend three grand getting it overturned!'

'Lola, I'm really sorry. I don't know what to say.... It'll be all right of course. You'll be all right. The baby will be lovely.'

'If I have it.'

I abort my enthusiasm.

'Ah, you're not sure...'

'Is anyone ever?'

I stop short of the obvious contradiction.

'I think I will have it. Don't know why.'

'*Do* have it. You don't need to know why.' I declare with all the freedom of someone not directly affected by the moral dilemma. Advice is such a luxury: I give it away all the time. Perhaps this is why no-one wants it.

'Lola, if there's anything I can do…'

'What can you do?' Lola amputates my blandishment.

'Well, I can…. I can….'

'Exactly…. Everyone's alone.'

My silence agrees implicitly, treacherously.

'My mother's ecstatic about it of course.' Laments Lola. 'Just what I need: another chance for that fucking madwoman to control my life!'

Suddenly, I want to leave there and then. Lola's right: I can't help. Truth be told, I don't really want to help. If only she knew I'm suffering from terminal selfishness rendering me incapable of interest in other people's problems past a certain stage. And the bar is hot, overbearingly airless. Suddenly I am choking on my own sense of impotence in the face of Lola's fate. What can I do? And if I can't do anything what's the point of talking about it?

But then, of course, talking about it is what we do precisely because we can't *do* anything about it. In fact, the less we can *do* about it, the more we *talk* about it. I could do nothing to help Lola and she couldn't do anything to help me. So we talked until closing time. Hugged, and as we hugged I thought of the new life dreaming in her womb. I never saw Lola again. Nor, I heard, did Ronnie.

### *142 – Phil the blackmailer*

This time, Phil the Janitor is not on his day off.

'Phil, can I have a word?'

I approach him in the depths of his domain in the bowels of the depot. He turns and looks at me dispassionately: perhaps I am only one of the several people he is blackmailing today - and not particularly high on his current list of priorities.

I challenge his indifference and my lowly place upon his blackmail list.

'I believe we've got something to talk about.'

'Is that a fact?'

'Yes, a certain photo – of someone in distress…'

'I wouldn't know anything about that. Seen one of a dirty fucker pretending to be a bus-driver, if that's what you mean!'

'Yes, Phil, that's the one I mean....'

Phil the janitor stands, mop raised in defiance, surrounded by rows of canisters and plastic containers, posed like his own private guard of minders.

'Apparently you know what I did last summer.' I venture. Perhaps gentlemanly irony would work its matey magic...

'I know you took a shit on Clapham Common,' sneers Phil.

'Yes. You do.' I confirm somewhat limply. I continue: 'The question is – what do you want to do about it?'

'I could ask you the same thing,' says Phil.

For a janitor, and without wishing to sound unduly snotty, Phil's game of verbal chess is surprisingly good. But I already have my next move up my sleeve.

We stand face-to-face – or should I say face-to-mop, because I am unarmed, whereas Phil is packing serious heat in the mop department.

A pause. I am just about to play my ace by treating Phil as a fellow human being and reasoning with him; thus, I hope, totally disarming his innate sense of umbrage. But then, for reasons not entirely clear to me, Phil the janitor goes up a gear. Indeed, Phil the janitor swept into moral mode.

'What sort of person shits in public? Disgusting, that's what you are!'

'I had no choice. I'm ill.'

'Tell me about it! Sick in the 'ead is what you are. Shitting! In public!'

I bat his disgust back at him, playing for time.

'So you're going to blackmail me: is that it? My shitting in public – even though I had no choice – that's disgusting; but blackmailing me: that's fine, is it?'

Phil the janitor bristles with all the bristly self-righteousness at his disposal.

'If it teaches you a lesson...'

Then I do something I don't normally do. I square up to the man with the mop.

Phil the janitor is big – but not that big. And he's sort of flabby too, like his morals. He looks flushed as I approach him, appropriately adjacent to the men's loos.

Truth to tell, I am genuinely angry for a moment; irate to find my dignity compromised so sanctimoniously by this, the least dignified man in the depot.

'Let me tell you, Phil: you're not going to teach me a lesson and you're not going to blackmail me. You know why? Because, first, I don't have anything to learn from you; and second, because you haven't got anything on me!'

'I've got photos!'

'Yes and so have I, because you sent them to me. And you know what I'm going to do with them? I'm going to post them round the depot myself! – With your name on them! Yeah, that's right: I'm going to tell people you took pictures of me while I was shitting as a result of colonic problems... then tried to blackmail me. Work that one out!'

Phil the janitor takes a mental step back in confusion to consider the logic of my statement..... as do I.

Phil calls my bluff and steps forward again.

'Who'd believe ya?' he inquires very reasonably – so reasonably, in fact, that it wrong-foots me again for a moment.

'Who *wouldn't*?' I stall for time.

'Who *would*?' Phil chimes in like a chronic double-act.

'Well you know what, Phil: it doesn't matter who would or wouldn't believe me!'

'And why is that?' retorts the mop-handed counsel for the prosecution.

Then I remember my absolute trump card, which I then place down on the table with executionary contempt:

'Oh Phil...' I almost want to cradle his cheeks and stroke his hair.

'Phil, Phil, Phil... because I'm leaving, you fucking half-wit...' The insult is gratuitous and I immediately regret it. Too late! Phil flinches, utterly taken aback. I await his recoil.

'You're what?' demands Phil, desperate to resist my logic's force.

'I'm leaving this fucking job!'

I look at Phil. He looks at me. A moment of utter incomprehension passes between us: two men from such sublimely different worlds, with not a word of common language shared – how are they to take their leave of each other in this moment of intense intimacy? I shake my head slightly and back away.

'You ain't 'eard the last of this!' Phil calls after me. 'You were a useless fucking driver anyway!'

In this, as in so many things, Phil is absolutely right, I have to laugh just as he substantiates his assessment.

'You should hear the lads talk about you! Wanker!'

### 143 – True to my word

True to my word, moving in the shadows of the depot over the next week, I post up a couple of photos of my Clapham common shit around its walls. Few take the time to look at them, fewer still to discriminate what is going on within the pixels of Phil the Janitor's shaky moral vision.

More importantly, the intense spirit of irony that operates tirelessly in the sphere of human intercourse arranges it perfectly, so that it is Phil the Janitor who has to take my photos down by order of the management – which embarrassing defeat he tries to mitigate with one further threat:

'I've put these on Clive's desk. I'm sure he'll want to see what sort of man he hired.'

### 144 – The art of oscillation

'So that's it then?' declares Kate, expecting no answer. She has listened to my contretemps with Phil the Janitor; about how I'd given him and his blackmail attempt the finger. Yes, she had listened and taken the news of my earlier-than-intended resignation, with its attendant risk of short-term moneylessness with her usual patience, exhibiting, indeed, the stillness of a woman long-practised in the art of fatalism.

'I'll take out a loan, before I leave – tide us over.' I assure her unconvincingly, knowing our credit score is already creaking with incredibility.

'No.' Then Kate pauses as if preparing to take the weight of her next pronouncement.

'You take care of him.'

'What - kill Phil?' I chuckled and checked in with Kate's expression. She wasn't smiling.

Had she finally lost it? Had the last year or so of living with my profoundly eccentric grasp of reality finally pushed Kate over the edge? Had she, unbeknownst to me, been brooding a psychosis which now emerged fully-fledged before me in the form of a desire to carry out an assassination?

'No, not Phil, Matt... Tom.

Ah, Herodian infanticide of the first born! I get it: kill our own son: But how would that help?

Then I see that Kate is visibly regretting the day she'd met me.

'Tom...' she intones the word like the single beat of a very grave drum. – 'You look after him. I'll go back to work. One of the designers has just left. I spoke to them last week. They'll take me back part-time'

'But...

'I can earn more in couple of days than you do in a week driving that fucking bus.'

I don't answer for a few moments.

'I'm still going back.'

'What?

'Why should I be pushed out by this twat? I'm gunna resign when it suits me, not Phil the fucking Janitor!'

### 145 – Sunlight in the depot

And so at last, next day, the voice of Nemesis is heard across the depot. The disembodied tones of irrefutable authority ring out over the PA:

"Would Matt Grant please attend the manager's office before leaving the depot please?' That's Matt Grant to Mr Bennett's, please...'

I pretend I haven't heard. Other drivers pretend they haven't heard, pretend they haven't seen the pictures of me shitting, strung out across the depot. But it's come: the time of reckoning has drawn nigh.

'Come in, sit down, Matt,' Clever Clive invites me to make my neck comfortable in his guillotine. 'Look, this is obviously a serious matter to which I am duty-bound to pay serious attention – no, please don't interrupt; this is not the time and place for a discussion,' he confirms. - Isn't it? I thought that was why I was here!

'Clive, can I just say, before anything else, that I'm resigning. I'll serve out the rest of the month, but that's it.' I then tell Clive all about my illness and the disaster of Clapham Common.

'Well I knew the job had taken its toll on you, that's why we let you have time off – three weeks is highly unusual I have to say! Why didn't you tell us what happened? We'd've done something. I mean, not for long; contracts are contracts, but we'd've cut you a couple of months of slack...half pay, of course; can't get round those rules...'

I wanted to reply that I needed a lifetime to get over the shitty job that had had made me so involuntarily shit myself. Then I mention the question of my adversary.

'Phil... the Janitor ---'

'Fuck Phil!' Clive cuts me off, 'Let me deal with him!

Then, disconcertingly, Clever Clive suddenly becomes very human in saying goodbye.

'No, don't blame you mate. Don't know how you lasted as long as you did actually! Most of 'em thought you'd be a first-week bottler...'

Ah the double-edge compliment – favourite weapon of, and wielded so skilfully by, the second-rate.

'No, it ain't a nice job any more, this. Used to be, believe it or not. Times've changed. Everyone's in such a fuckin' 'urry, 'n't they? No, yer fare-paying public are an impatient bunch of arseholes by and large – with exceptions, of course. Well, upwards and onwards, Matt. Good luck mate. Hope things work out...'

And with that Clever Clive and I shake hands for the second and last time in our meaningless and yet strangely unforgettable relationship.

Walking down the drabbest of drab corridors in a drab depot on Drab street, Drabstown at drab o'clock, I suddenly registered that Clever Clive had prefaced – always did preface - everything he said with the word 'no'; as if life itself had become an essentially negative experience to which Clive had learned to say 'no' before agreeing to its dictates anyway. Clever Clive would never resign – precisely because Clever Clive had always been - resigned....

## 146 – Buddha in the high street

Strangely enough, the fortnight that follows is the calmest I've ever driven. It's all in the mind – life, I mean. Now I know I'm leaving this job, I can do it – well, for the next couple of weeks....

Of course, as a lover of melodrama, I decided not just to resign, but resign in style. How to do this with a big red bus? Surely the possibilities were endless? Ironically, no – at least not without causing serious hardship to a great deal of people in the act – and this my conscience sadly would not let me do.

Not that I didn't test my theoretical capacity for revenge as I drove out my final weeks of duty on the bus. Donna, with her red Celtic roots now showing through the gothic black dye, and with that penchant for understatement which I had come to recognise as her psychological trademark, suggested I set my bus on fire on London Bridge. My own favourite option for a week or two was to stop my bus just past Threadneedle Street, get out and just walk off, thus plunging the whole Square Mile – and hopefully the financial system itself - into daylong confusion (possibly shitting outside my former office into the bargain; having, of course, become an expert in the art of the public dump).

This would have been wonderful. I did seriously consider it. - But what if the emergency services suddenly needed to get through that street? Or if some innocent member of the public were desperate to get help to or from someone else; or to get to some vital meeting, romantic tryst or destination? No, that would never do; and then, ultimately, the possibility of being sent to prison afterwards also weighed against the act.

Then what about crashing the bus with no-one on board, say late at night? Or colliding in some strangely terminal way with the depot, imprisoning all its workers and shutting it down indefinitely? Yes, yes, all very appealing in their own ultimately unworkable way; but then, one morning, the manner of my departure was determined for me.

As my time at the wheel drew to a matter of a few remaining days, I turned into one of those shabby-chic roads behind Victoria station; well, not so much behind as between Victoria and Chelsea, and thus claimed by neither; some call it by the exotic, almost mythic, Hesperidean name of Pimlico: a strange no-man's land of irregular buildings, domiciles and inhabitants wherein the penurious lie down cheek-by-jowl with the prosperous; where counts fallen on hard times, and council tenants never risen from them, brush curious shoulders in the street.

In this particular avenue, it became clear another bus had got here before me – and wasn't leaving any time soon, since it had come to a dead stop outside one of those recherché antiques emporia that serve the laughably variable tastes of the terminally rich.

Directed by police alongside the stationary bus I became aware of a golden figure standing in the road with one arm raised as if to stop oncoming traffic, which feat he had achieved most gracefully. Edging my bus slowly past the group of men and women dealing with this golden impasse I saw that there was not one but three such golden figures involved and mingling, as it were, with the gathered, well-heeled throng. The other two gilded figures were standing, their hands posed in various gestures of peaceful challenge, on a traffic island, as if directing passers-by – but none were passing by. For all had stopped to gaze at what they saw. And then I saw one more figure...

Or half of one: a life-size, Chinese porcelain Bodhisattva, his beautiful head and torso emerging, as if born forth miraculously in brilliant painted red from the dark black asphalt of the street. Above the hubbub I heard the tortured sound of a woman's crying. Suddenly it was clear the Bodhisattva's emergence had shattered not only the atmosphere of normality but also his own body, the rest of which lay dispersed around him in a thousand irreparable pieces across the road.

A van carrying all four priceless bodhisattvas had apparently backed out in front of the bus, its rear doors sprung open by the vicious impact, thereby ejecting the three surviving golden gilded wooden Buddhas (quickly retrieved) but also the porcelain Manchu dynasty Bodhisattva intent on self-sacrifice.

Such was the jigsaw of Enlightenment I saw before me. A life-size, Chinese porcelain Bodhisattva dedicating himself to the salvation of every living being, prepared, as it were, to sacrifice himself – in this case, in an intervention between the spirit of commerce and the London traffic – in order to secure human happiness...

The woman continued to cry in a foreign language – Italian, the owner, as I later read, of the broken Bodhisattva, bewailing her loss; though he himself only smiled as he lay superbly fractured, cut in jagged half, such was the power of his contentment, his peace of mind was, itself, so deep it knew no sundering.

Nevertheless, to those of mortal thoughts there lay in a street in Pimlico two centuries of culture shattered irretrievably in an instant.

'Move along, there's nothing to see,' said the traffic copper in flagrant contradiction of the facts. For in truth there was everything to see. In this one instant, in this street in Pimlico all opposites converged: an instantaneous collision of high culture with low commerce; of timeless wisdom and comically bad timing; indeed, of high tragedy and low farce; of the simple 'mechanicals' of policemen with the sage beauty of the Bodhisattva; of banal purpose with divine intent; of the statue's irreparable brokenness compared with the Bodhisattva's unbreakable composure; of his eternal smile contrasting with his owner's tears at approximately ten past five that afternoon...

As I drove home that night on one of my last round-trips back to the depot the images of the day impressed themselves upon my mind with meaning.

I have been broken more than once myself. Heartbreak, breakdown; we all know the words, have all felt the mental and emotional muscles tear. Indeed, what was the event in Auckland Avenue if not a celebration of the power of broken-ness, of the forced breakage of one way of life and its eventual replacement by another? The porcelain Manchu Bodhisattva somehow conveyed that only brokenness is permanent; only breakage is reliable; that it is the fracture of our artificially frozen forms that releases all the atomic energy we are too terrified to access; energy we usually only experience in the internal atomic bomb of pain, loss, death and separation. The smile of the fractured porcelain Bodhisattva, however, seemed to say it is possible to experience brokenness in another way....

On my last day, I saw there was no need for a grand gesture in my mode of resignation. In taking on the job all those months ago, in taking on the mantle of my illness and casting it off again; in being forced to confront the need to resign and find some other way; in confronting Big Len, Clever Clive and Phil the janitor albeit unwittingly, I had already careered into my future; had, unbeknownst to me, already crashed the bus.

## 147 – Epilogue - Grand gestures in small moments

Life comes to a head and at that moment you realise that, for better or for worse, you are intensely alive; that life, whether you like it or not, always has its own way of coming - is supposed to come - to a head: your head, my head, a porcelain Buddha's head.... We supply the fragile china; life drives the bus right through it.

And there is something mystical in the splinter and fragmentation. We may fear it, but something in us also loves release. In this we are disciples of Dionysus, whether we've heard the name or not. Our element is our energy: energy expressed, energy repressed, energy concealed in hearts, released in rapture, congealed in depression, contained in objects of desire – where does the desire go when you at last possess the object! – Energy in tears, laughter, song, energy in colour and form – with such energies as these we strike the red-hot archetype upon the anvil; in these we shape our souls – and in small intimate occasions just as much as our more spectacular events. Indeed, the grand gesture often expresses itself to us best in a moment of great subtlety. Not that one necessarily knows beforehand exactly how such subtlety will manifest.

At the end of that last day, having kissed Donna, my favourite Goth bus driver, a temporary goodbye, I made sure the depot was empty – well, maybe Phil the janitor was skulking further off, it didn't matter. Actually, his presence as the underlying, vaguely malicious spirit of banality, the guardian of sub-audible discontent, was somehow poetically appropriate as I folded up my high-vis jacket and my uniform. I turned to look just one last time at that dowdy room painted in the mute nicotine-stained colours of despondency. I replaced the fob of keys reserved for bus 190, slowly the swinging pendulum of keys lost their last impetus and settled, as the hands of gravity's clock demand, at an eternal half past six upon the hook.

Returning home that evening I found Kate sketching at her drawing board, haloed by concentration and shielded by a silence I did not challenge. It was eerily quiet in the flat. Maybe something to do with that night's supermoon: its weird, influential light flooded in at the window, insisting on possibilities of illumination other than nature's incandescence.

Sitting down with the laptop, I looked around to make sure the baby monitor was working, then remembered we no longer used it anymore. Without resisting arrest, Tom had gone reasonably peaceably to bed, and, in a slow, secret upturn in both our fortunes more revolutionary than we then had power to recognise, now slept uninterruptedly through the night. I closed my laptop and went upstairs to kiss him, but approaching his bed, got distracted by the moon at the window again: so proximate and familiar, so remote and inhuman - why would we not project a spirit and character upon this otherwise diminutive, dead satellite that revolves around us so faithfully? It's such a quintessentially human thing to do – and infinitely more affirmative than any mere analysis of its matter.

And so the moon gazed down: man or woman (or both), I thought I read in its face an expression of quizzical indulgence, as though almost surprised somehow by the luminous tranquillity of the nocturnal London gardens down below. Taking great care not to wake my son, I gently kissed his forehead and went downstairs, leaving him dreaming by the vigil light of the moon.

∞

*Crash the Bus*

*James Murphy*

© **2015 Heretics Press**

**All rights reserved.**

*James Murphy*

© 2015 Heretics Press

All rights reserved.

www.ingramcontent.com/pod-product-compliance
Lightning Source LLC
Chambersburg PA
CBHW062128170626
46813CB00002B/603